SLIP SLIDING AWAY

The crack of a lightning bolt and the thunder that accompanied it pounded at Longarm's ears as the bolt struck a tree on top of the hill. The searing flash lasted only a second, but it was enough to show Longarm the figure looming above him. One of the outlaws was slogging up the hill in the rain and mud, probably trying to reach the gang's horses and check on them.

The man saw Longarm at the same time and bellowed, "He's up here! Damn it, he's up here!"

Then the gun in his hand spouted flame as he hammered slugs at the lawman.

Desperately, Longarm rolled to the side as the slugs pounded into the mud where he had been a fraction of a second earlier. He reached across his body to the cross-draw rig where he kept the Colt and pulled the gun. It bucked and roared in his hand as he came to a stop on his back.

The bullet tore up at an angle through the outlaw's body and knocked him off his feet. He landed on his back and slid down the hill on the slippery mud.

Longarm heard yells and shots and knew the rest of the gang had heard the shouted warning. He tried to jump to his feet, but as he did, his boots slipped in the mud and he sat down hard. Almost before he knew what was happening, he was sliding, too, straight down the hillside into the teeth of the outlaws' guns . . .

DON'T MISS THESE
ALL-ACTION WESTERN SERIES
FROM THE BERKLEY PUBLISHING GROUP

THE GUNSMITH by J. R. Roberts

Clint Adams was a legend among lawmen, outlaws, and ladies. They called him . . . the Gunsmith.

LONGARM by Tabor Evans

The popular long-running series about Deputy U.S. Marshal Long—his life, his loves, his fight for justice.

SLOCUM by Jake Logan

Today's longest-running action Western. John Slocum rides a deadly trail of hot blood and cold steel.

BUSHWHACKERS by B. J. Lanagan

An action-packed series by the creators of Longarm! The rousing adventures of the most brutal gang of cutthroats ever assembled—Quantrill's Raiders.

DIAMONDBACK by Guy Brewer

Dex Yancey is Diamondback, a Southern gentleman turned con man when his brother cheats him out of the family fortune. Ladies love him. Gamblers hate him. But nobody pulls one over on Dex . . .

WILDGUN by Jack Hanson

The blazing adventures of mountain man Will Barlow—from the creators of Longarm!

TEXAS TRACKER by Tom Calhoun

Meet J.T. Law: the most relentless—and dangerous—man-hunter in all Texas. Where sheriffs and posses fail, he's the best man to bring in the most vicious outlaws—for a price.

TABOR EVANS

LONGARM

AND THE OWLHOOTS'
GRAVEYARD

JOVE BOOKS, NEW YORK

THE BERKLEY PUBLISHING GROUP
Published by the Penguin Group
Penguin Group (USA) Inc.
375 Hudson Street, New York, New York 10014, USA
Penguin Group (Canada), 90 Eglinton Avenue East, Suite 700, Toronto, Ontario M4P 2Y3, Canada
(a division of Pearson Penguin Canada Inc.)
Penguin Books Ltd., 80 Strand, London WC2R 0RL, England
Penguin Group Ireland, 25 St. Stephen's Green, Dublin 2, Ireland (a division of Penguin Books Ltd.)
Penguin Group (Australia), 250 Camberwell Road, Camberwell, Victoria 3124, Australia
(a division of Pearson Australia Group Pty. Ltd.)
Penguin Books India Pvt. Ltd., 11 Community Centre, Panchsheel Park, New Delhi—110 017, India
Penguin Group (NZ), Cnr. Airborne and Rosedale Roads, Albany, Auckland 1310, New Zealand
(a division of Pearson New Zealand Ltd.)
Penguin Books (South Africa) (Pty.) Ltd., 24 Sturdee Avenue, Rosebank, Johannesburg 2196,
South Africa

Penguin Books Ltd., Registered Offices: 80 Strand, London WC2R 0RL, England

This is a work of fiction. Names, characters, places, and incidents either are the product of the author's imagination or are used fictitiously, and any resemblance to actual persons, living or dead, business establishments, events, or locales is entirely coincidental.

LONGARM AND THE OWLHOOTS' GRAVEYARD

A Jove Book / published by arrangement with the author

PRINTING HISTORY
Jove edition / July 2006

Copyright © 2006 by The Berkley Publishing Group.

ISBN: 0-515-14157-7

JOVE®
Jove Books are published by The Berkley Publishing Group,
a division of Penguin Group (USA) Inc.,
375 Hudson Street, New York, New York 10014.
JOVE is a registered trademark of Penguin Group (USA) Inc.
The "J" design is a trademark belonging to Penguin Group (USA) Inc.

PRINTED IN THE UNITED STATES OF AMERICA

10   9   8   7   6   5   4   3   2   1

Chapter 1

Longarm dropped to one knee and fired twice. Then as bullets ripped through the air beside his head, he flung himself to the ground and rolled behind a nearby rock. Lead whined off stone as the outlaws continued blazing away at him.

There had to be an easier way to make a living, instead of getting shot at on a regular basis by killers, counterfeiters, bank robbers, horse thieves, and rustlers. Why, he could be wearing an apron and clerking in a store back in Denver right now, instead of hunkering behind a rock on an isolated West Texas hillside while a bunch of no-good desperadoes tried to kill him.

Problem was, to a man like Longarm, wearing an apron and clerking in a store would just be a slower, more agonizing way of getting dead.

Not only that, but he was too damned old and set in his ways to change. He raised up enough to snap a couple of shots at the clump of boulders farther up the hill where the gang had taken cover. Then he ducked down again and listened to the bullets smashing into the rock in front of him.

He was in a pickle, all right. The army mount he had picked up at Fort Sam Houston in San Antonio had run off down the hill, taking Longarm's Winchester with him. There was no cover for a good fifty yards on either side of

1

him, and nothing between him and the rocks where Hathaway's gang was holed up. He had a couple dozen cartridges in his coat pocket, but once those were gone he was up Shit Creek without a paddle.

And on top of all that, it was fixing to rain.

A black cloud loomed over the top of the hill. Jagged fingers of lightning clawed their way through the roiling sable mass. The frequent rumble of thunder was like the sound of distant drums. A chilly wind blew over the hillside, kicking up dust devils and dispelling the heat of what had been a typical summer day in West Texas.

Rain was downright rare in these parts, but when it did come, a-cloud, the storm was usually a gullywasher and a toad-strangler. Arroyos that had been bone-dry for months could turn into raging rivers in a matter of minutes. More than one unwary pilgrim had camped in some sandy draw and been washed away by a flash flood.

There was no threat of that here; Longarm and the men trying to kill him were too far up on the hillside for that. But they might be in for a downpour, a nice, blinding downpour.

Longarm's mouth stretched into a grin under the sweeping longhorn mustaches as he realized that the approaching thunderstorm might be his only chance to come out of this ambush alive.

He had been on the trail of Nate Hathaway and his gang for a couple of weeks now, ever since being given the job by his boss, Chief Marshal Billy Vail up in Denver. Hathaway's bunch had held up several banks and stagecoaches and trains across Arkansas, Louisiana, and Texas, but when they robbed an army payroll wagon, they had become Uncle Sam's business and, ultimately, Longarm's chore.

After picking up their trail in San Antonio, he had followed them northwest. He thought he had them cornered in Junction City, but then Hathaway had pulled a fast one and taken off for the tall and uncut with the loot while leaving his partners behind to deal with Longarm.

2

That had been a bloody little shoot-out while it lasted, resulting in a couple of dead owlhoots and four more on the run. Up there on the hill above Longarm were Wally Brewster, Con Haney, and the Padgett brothers, Lew and Hank. It was a toss-up who they wanted dead more—the federal lawman dogging their trail or their double-crossing former leader. Longarm figured they had set up this ambush for him primarily to keep him from getting to Hathaway first. They didn't want anybody interfering with the vengeance they planned to take on their ex-partner.

Longarm didn't much care who actually ventilated the son of a bitch; he just wanted that army payroll back. And, of course, to bring the entire gang to justice one way or the other. A couple of them had already bitten the dust, back in Junction City, and he had wired Billy Vail to that effect, adding that he was continuing with his pursuit of the others.

If he died on this lonely hillside, would Vail ever know about it? Or would Longarm join the ranks of countless other lawmen who had gone out in pursuit of owlhoots, only to never return, their unburied and unmourned bones bleaching in the harsh frontier sun?

He had to stop thinking like that. Fat drops of rain began to spatter down around him as he reloaded the Colt. He still had a chance, as long as it rained hard enough. One of the drops struck the back of Longarm's hand, and it hit with sufficient force to sting.

Less than a minute later, the heavens opened up.

Although it was only the middle of the afternoon, the sky turned almost as black as night. Rain poured down, whipped sideways by the howling wind. In just a few seconds, Longarm was soaked to the skin. His slicker was on that blasted horse, too, along with his rifle. The rain fell so hard and thick that when he raised up to look over the rock, he couldn't see more than a few feet. The clump of boulders where the gang was hidden was completely invisible.

Which meant those bastards couldn't see him anymore, either.

3

He holstered his gun and moved to the side, staying low. He couldn't hear any shots over the sluicing roar of the rain, but that didn't mean the outlaws were holding their fire. They might still be shooting down the hill, toward where they thought he was. He didn't want to get hit by a stray bullet.

Water splashed around his hands and knees as he crawled across the hillside. When he had gone about fifty yards, he stopped and turned, then started crawling up the hill. The slope was the only thing that allowed him to keep himself oriented. Otherwise, he couldn't really tell where he was in this blinding downpour.

The outlaws had been about a hundred yards above him on the hillside. When Longarm estimated that he had gone farther than that, he turned again and started crawling back the direction he had come from. If the gang was still holed up in the rocks, he ought to be moving above and behind them now. Of course, there was no guarantee that they hadn't changed position, too.

It seemed to Longarm that the rain wasn't falling quite as hard now. That came as no surprise. These West Texas cloudbursts often didn't last very long. Sometimes, in fact, they stopped as quickly as they began. The runoff was still rolling like a river down the hill, though.

The crack of a lightning bolt and the thunder that accompanied it pounded at Longarm's ears as the bolt struck a tree on top of the hill. The searing flash lasted only a second, but it was enough to show Longarm the figure looming above him. One of the outlaws was slogging up the hill in the rain and mud, probably trying to reach the gang's horses and check on them.

The man saw Longarm at the same time and bellowed, "He's up here! Damn it, he's up here!"

Then the gun in his hand spouted flame as he hammered slugs at the lawman.

4

Chapter 2

Desperately, Longarm rolled to the side as the slugs pounded into the mud where he had been a fraction of a second earlier. He reached across his body to the cross-draw rig where he kept the Colt and pulled the gun. It bucked and roared in his hand as he came to a stop on his back.

The bullet tore up at an angle through the outlaw's body and knocked him off his feet. He landed on his back and slid down the hill on the slippery mud.

Longarm heard yells and shots and knew the rest of the gang had heard the shouted warning. He tried to jump to his feet, but as he did, his boots slipped in the mud and he sat down hard. Almost before he knew what was happening, he was sliding, too, straight down the hillside into the teeth of the outlaws' guns.

Since he couldn't stop himself, he decided to try to turn this misadventure into an advantage. The slope was pretty steep, and he was going fast. He saw muzzle flashes in the rain and returned the fire. He was among the gang in little more than a heartbeat, taking them completely by surprise.

Longarm didn't come to a stop until the soles of his boots jolted against one of the boulders where the outlaws had taken cover. A bullet spanked off the rock above him as he rolled over onto his belly. He had thumbed cartridges into all six chambers of the Colt's cylinder when he reloaded, and he thought he had a couple of rounds left.

He drew a bead on a gray shape rushing toward him and pulled the trigger. Flame lanced from the barrel of the gun. The shape doubled over and fell. Longarm held his fire. He didn't know if any of the outlaws were left, or if he had gotten them all.

Breathing shallowly, he listened to the rain. It definitely wasn't falling as hard now. He could see maybe twenty feet. His keen eyes made out a couple of crumpled, motionless shapes on the ground, with runoff swirling around them. Longarm was pretty sure those two were either dead or wounded badly enough that they were out of the fight. He thought he had done for the first one, higher up the slope, too.

But that left the fourth man, and Longarm couldn't see or hear him anywhere.

The son of a bitch had gone to ground. Longarm was convinced of that. The fourth outlaw was out there somewhere, lurking, waiting for a shot at the big lawman. Or he might be sneaking up right now, and Longarm wouldn't be able to hear him because of the rain.

Stay still or move again? Longarm asked himself that question as he lay there on his belly, water running around him. He was cold and soaked and miserable, but that would be the case no matter what he did. He decided to stay where he was and make the remaining owlhoot come to him.

Minutes ticked past with maddening slowness. The rain let up even more as the worst of the storm moved on to the south, taking the thunder and lightning with it. The flashes still lit up the sky, but not with the same blinding intensity. The thunder no longer exploded; it was back to a rumble, that distant drum sound again. And while the rain fell steadily, it wasn't a downpour anymore.

Longarm heard something—a tiny jingling sound, followed by a scrape. Somebody's spur had just hit against rock.

And the sound came from *above* him.

The bastard was on top of the boulder.

Longarm rolled to his right and saw the dark shape plummeting down at him. The outlaw's long duster billowed out around him like wings. He let out a screeching yell at he dove at the lawman.

Longarm triggered his final shot but couldn't tell if he hit the man or not. The outlaw landed halfway on top of him. The knife in the man's hand dug into the muddy ground, missing Longarm's head by scant inches. Longarm clamped his fingers around the wrist of the outlaw's knife hand and swung his other arm in a punch at the man's head. The blow landed, but not solidly, grazing along the side of the man's skull above his ear.

The outlaw panted curses as he wrestled with Longarm, trying to get his free hand on Longarm's throat. Longarm held him off and drove his knee up into the man's belly. Sour breath gusted in Longarm's face.

Both men were covered with mud, which made it hard for them to get a grip on each other. Longarm twisted the outlaw's wrist until the man yelled in pain and let go of the knife, but the next moment, the man had slipped behind him somehow and got an arm around Longarm's neck. As pressure from that arm closed down on Longarm's throat, the man forced him facedown into the mud.

Longarm sputtered and choked and thought that he was damned if he was going to let himself be drowned halfway up a hill like this. He drove an elbow back into the man's midsection and then heaved himself upward, arching off the ground and throwing his opponent off to one side.

Mud still clogged Longarm's nose and mouth as he scrambled up. He kicked the outlaw hard in the belly and then in the chest. That gave him a moment's respite. He stepped back and wiped the mud away from his face so he could breathe again.

The outlaw was curled up in a ball, in pain from those kicks. The rain had washed away enough of the mud so that Longarm recognized the rawboned features of Hank Padgett.

Padgett glared up at Longarm with utter hatred. "You damn . . . lawdog!" he gasped. "I'll kill you!"

"Not likely, old son," Longarm told him wearily.

But then Padgett reached down into the mud beside him and came up with the knife he had dropped a minute earlier. Longarm hadn't seen it in the muck, but Padgett had. The outlaw's arm drew back.

Longarm recalled that Padgett was supposed to be damned good with a knife. He could throw one with deadly accuracy, and with enough force to drive the blade through a half-inch-thick board. It would sure as hell penetrate flesh and muscle.

And not only was Padgett too far away for Longarm to reach him before he could throw, but the lawman's Colt was somewhere down there in the mud, too, and empty to boot.

But he wasn't unarmed. Even as Padgett drew back the knife to throw it, Longarm's hand flashed under his coat to his watch chain. He pulled it out, and welded to one end of it was the little .41-caliber derringer that had saved his bacon more than once.

The deadly little gun cracked and spat flame. Padgett was driven backward by the slug just as he began his throw. The knife went up in the air and then came down to splash harmlessly into the mud.

The derringer held two rounds, so Longarm kept it trained on Padgett as he approached the outlaw. Padgett had both hands pressed to his chest where the bullet had struck him. Blood welled between his fingers, only to be washed away by the still steadily falling rain.

"You . . . you've killed me!" he gasped.

"Reckon that's what you had planned for me, Padgett," said Longarm, with no sympathy in his voice. He knew that Padgett had gunned down at least four innocent people during the course of the gang's robberies.

"L-lucky son of a bitch!" Blood trickled from the corners of Padgett's mouth now. "We should've . . . had you!"

"The lucky one's Nate Hathaway," Longarm said. "He had all five of us after him, but now I'm the only one left to see that he gets what's coming to him."

Longarm didn't know for sure that the other three outlaws were dead, but he wanted Padgett to think so. If the man had any leads to where Hathaway was, Longarm wanted to know about them.

"Don't mention that . . . double-crosser's name," Padgett grated. His voice was weaker now. He was fading. As he spoke again, Longarm had to lean over him to make out what he was saying. Padgett asked, "What's your . . . name?"

"It's Long. Deputy U.S. Marshal Custis Long."

"Marshal . . . you gotta promise me . . . you'll get Nate for us . . . Make the bastard . . . suffer."

"You know where I can find him?" Longarm asked.

"We heard a rumor . . . he was headed for . . . a place called . . . Lodestone—"

Those were Hank Padgett's last words. His head sagged back, and his hands fell away from the bloody, black-rimmed bullethole in his chest. He stared up sightlessly into the rain.

Longarm straightened. He had never heard of the settlement Padgett had mentioned, but if there was a chance Nate Hathaway was there, he would find the place.

"Lodestone," Longarm repeated aloud, and in the distance sounded an ominous roll of thunder.

Chapter 3

Not surprisingly, the rain stopped completely a few minutes later, and not long after that, the clouds broke and the sun came out and the day started heating up again.

Only now it was more miserable than ever because the air was so steamy. In fact, while he was checking on the bodies of the other outlaws, Longarm saw tendrils of steam rising from some of the rocks that had been heated up by the sun earlier in the day.

Brewster, Haney, and Lew Padgett were all dead, just like Hank Padgett. Hank had called Longarm lucky, and he knew that was true. Downing four owlhoots like that and not receiving a scratch in return was well-nigh miraculous. Longarm had learned a long time ago, though, not to turn his nose up at good fortune. A man in his line of work needed all the lucky breaks he could get.

He fished his six-gun out of the mud and trudged down the muddy hill, leaving the dead outlaws where they lay. Longarm's horse had retreated a couple of hundred yards when the shooting started, after Longarm dove out of the saddle. He hadn't known that the critter was so damned gun-shy. That was surprising considering that it was an army mount. Maybe that was why that sergeant at the stables back at Fort Sam Houston had been smiling. The horse stood watching him nervously as he approached, but at least it didn't run off again and Longarm was grateful for that.

He got a cloth from his saddlebags and started cleaning the gun. He was covered with mud, too, but it was more important to get the gun back in good working order. When that was done and the Colt was reloaded, then Longarm used the cloth to wipe away some of the sticky mud from his face.

The outlaws' mounts were still tied at the top of the hill. Longarm went up to get them a few minutes later. He led the horses down the slope and one by one lifted the corpses, slung each one over the back of a horse, and tied the bodies in place. The horses didn't care for carrying dead men, but Longarm spoke softly to them and kept them calmed down enough so that they didn't bolt.

Of course, the easiest thing would have been to leave the bodies here for the coyotes and the buzzards, and such a fate was about what the owlhoots had coming to them. Longarm figured he could take them on to Lodestone, though, and see that they got a proper burial, whether they deserved it or not.

Besides, there was probably a lawman of some sort in Lodestone, maybe even a telegraph office. If so, Longarm could wire Billy Vail, and the local badge could back up his story about the members of the gang being dead.

And when he rode in, leading horses carrying four corpses, word was bound to get around town. If Nate Hathaway *was* there, the news might spook him into running, in which case he would draw attention to himself and Longarm could follow him. Or he might just try to kill the big lawman, and that would be all right with Longarm, too. Let Hathaway come to him.

Once he had the corpses loaded, he gathered the reins, swung up into his saddle, and rode out, still headed northwest. That was the way the gang had been going, so he figured Lodestone was probably in that direction, too.

The wet, muddy clothes chafed at Longarm. They stunk, too. Brown tweed just didn't smell that good when it got soaked. He had clean pairs of underwear and jeans and a shirt in his saddlebags, but he didn't want to put on clean clothes when he was so dirty otherwise. He was resigned to letting the sun dry his outfit, even though that might take a long time as wet as it was.

But a short time later when he spotted a line of cottonwoods in front of him, he knew he was coming to a creek, and he decided he might be able to stop and clean up there.

The outlaws certainly weren't in any hurry. They had already gotten as far as they were going to go.

Longarm reined in and dismounted and tied all the horses to one of the trees. The creek ran between grassy banks and was about ten feet wide. It was running a little muddy because of the rain, but Longarm figured it would at least get him cleaner than he was. He hung his gunbelt on the saddle and started taking his clothes off.

When he was naked, he waded out into the stream, which was about three feet deep at its deepest point. He carried his clothes with him. Bending over, he began scrubbing the mud off of them. When he had them as clean as he could get them, he spread them out on the bank to dry and turned his attention to himself. He sat down in the creek and ducked his head under the surface.

The horses grazed while Longarm was bathing. The corpses didn't do anything. Longarm washed as much of the mud off as he could, although he knew he would still feel a little gritty until he got a chance to take a real bath. When he was finished, he stood up and shook himself off like a dog. He ran his fingers through his hair, trying to comb the wet tangle.

That was when he heard the hoofbeats and looked around to see a buggy rolling toward the creek from the east.

Being surprised like that was disconcerting enough, but it was even worse when Longarm realized a second later that the driver of the buggy was a woman. There were a few trees between him and her, but they were spaced out enough so that they didn't provide much of a screen. He lunged up onto the bank and hurried over to his horse, then fumbled in the saddlebags for those clean clothes.

He had gotten the long underwear bottoms pulled up around his lean shanks when the woman called cheerfully from the other side of the creek, "Don't hurry on my account, sir."

He turned to see that she had brought the buggy to a stop on the opposite bank and was sitting there with a mischievous smile on her face. It was a mighty pretty face, too, topped by auburn curls. She wore a bottle green traveling outfit, and a hat of the same shade perched on her hair.

"Ma'am, I'd take it kindly if you could give me a mite of privacy," Longarm said.

"Yes, I suppose that would be the proper thing to do," she said, but he noticed she wasn't getting in any hurry to turn away or even avert her eyes from his half-dressed state. Finally, though, she stepped down from the buggy and turned her back. "Let me know when you're decent, sir."

Longarm pulled on the denim trousers and then shrugged into a butternut shirt with a bib front. He hadn't had a chance to dry off when he got out of the creek, so now *these* clothes were damp, too. But at least they weren't soaked and it probably wouldn't take long for them to dry.

"All right, ma'am," he said as he tucked the shirttail into his trousers.

She turned, and now her face wore a concerned expression. "I'm sorry," she said. "I really didn't mean to intrude."

"That's all right, ma'am. It ain't like I've got any claim on this creek. Folks have a right to go wherever they want. It's a free country, after all."

"Yes, but that doesn't free one from the restraints of common courtesy." A smile flashed again on her face. "It's

14

just that I don't often get a chance to see such a handsome specimen of unadorned masculinity."

Longarm wasn't sure he liked being referred to as any kind of specimen, but he let it pass. "Reckon we ought to introduce ourselves," he said. "My name's Custis Long."

He left out any mention of being a deputy United States marshal. That was just habitual caution on his part. Some folks got skittish when they knew he was a lawman, even when they hadn't done anything wrong.

"I'm Caroline Thaxter. Miss Caroline Thaxter."

Longarm nodded politely. "Pleased to meet you, ma'am."

Caroline Thaxter looked past him, and the smile suddenly disappeared from her face, along with most of the color. Longarm knew without asking that she had just noticed the four bodies on the horses. She must not have noticed them before now because they were in the shadows under the cottonwood trees.

"Are . . . are those men *dead*?"

"Yes, ma'am, they are." Longarm thought about saying he was sorry, but of course he really wasn't. He didn't regret ridding the world of four such vicious hardcases.

"Did you . . . kill them?"

Looked like he was going to have to either lie or tell her who he really was. He said, "Yes, ma'am, I did, but it's all right. I'm a lawman. Deputy U.S. marshal, in fact."

"That . . . that's good. I suppose." She swallowed hard. "I've never seen . . . I mean, I've seen dead bodies before, of course, at funerals, but . . . I never . . ."

"It's all right, ma'am, I understand. Just to ease your mind, you ought to know that these were bad men, outlaws, and I had to kill 'em in the course of my duties as a law officer. Fact of the matter is, they bushwhacked me because they knew I was on their trail."

"I see." Caroline was carefully looking away from the corpses now. "And after killing them, you stopped to . . . bathe?"

"Yes, ma'am. I was soaked and covered with mud. Got caught in that thunderstorm that passed through earlier this afternoon."

"Yes, I missed the storm. It passed west of my location." She paused. "What are you going to . . . do with them?"

"I've heard there's a settlement near here called Lodestone," Longarm said, not going into detail about who he'd heard it from or the circumstances under which he had heard it. "I thought I'd take them in there, turn them over to the undertaker, and let the local law know what happened. Maybe wire my boss in Denver if there's a telegraph office."

"There's not," Caroline said. "I happen to know that. If there had been a telegraph office, I wouldn't be on my way there myself. I would have just sent a wire."

Longarm's eyebrows lifted in surprise. "You're bound for Lodestone, too, Miss Thaxter?"

"Yes, I am, Marshal. I suppose you could say that we're coming from different directions, you and I, but we have the same destination in mind."

"Yes, ma'am. You're traveling by yourself?"

She nodded. "That's right. I took the train to Trickham and rented this buggy there. I was told there's no stage to Lodestone. It's rather isolated, from what I hear."

"But you didn't mind setting out across country by your lonesome?"

Caroline's chin lifted rather defiantly. "I've never been one to let a little hardship stop me from doing what I need to do."

"I ain't talking about hardship so much as I am danger."

"I thought all the wild Indians were gone from this part of Texas."

"They are," Longarm agreed. "You got to go farther west, out to the Big Bend country, before you have to start worrying about Apaches coming up from below the Rio Grande to raid. The Comanch used to roam in these parts, but they're all up on the reservation now and have been for four or five years. I'm talking more about gents like those." He jerked a thumb toward the horses with their grisly burdens. "You wouldn't want to cross trails with men like that."

"I've heard that a decent woman is always safe with Western men, no matter how bad they might be otherwise."

"And that's true nine times out of ten," Longarm said with a nod. "It's that tenth time you got to worry about."

Caroline summoned up a smile. "Well, I don't have to worry anymore, because now I can go on to Lodestone with you, Mr. Long. I don't think anyone will bother me while I have a U.S. marshal for an escort."

Longarm hadn't made the offer yet, but that was just what he had in mind. He said, "It'll be my pleasure, ma'am, and I'll be right happy for the company. That is, if you don't mind traveling with . . ." He inclined his head toward the corpses.

Caroline Thaxter paled again for a moment. "Perhaps I should drive a short distance in front of you and the, ah, horses."

"Yes, ma'am," Longarm said. "I reckon that'd be a good idea."

Chapter 4

Longarm put on his socks and boots, buckled his gunbelt around his hips, and brushed the mud off his flat-crowned, snuff brown Stetson. The mud on the hat had dried, and the Stetson didn't look too bad after Longarm cleaned it up, just stained a mite. He would have it cleaned for real the next time he came across a haberdashery, but Lord knew when that would be. He was willing to bet they wouldn't have one in Lodestone.

Caroline Thaxter knew more about where to find the place than he did. She had gotten good directions when she rented the buggy in Trickham. So Longarm let her take the lead after they'd found a place where she could ford the creek in the buggy.

They headed closer to due west than Longarm had been going, so he thought that maybe it had been another stroke of luck that he'd run into Caroline. A mite embarrassing for a minute, when he'd been standing there buck naked in the creek, but lucky nevertheless.

Off to the north and northeast he could see a range of low, rounded peaks that he figured to be the Brady Mountains. Even farther in the distance, beyond the mountains, was the blue line of the Callahan Divide, which separated the watersheds of the Brazos and Colorado Rivers. Slightly

19

northwest was the valley of the Concho River, where Fort Concho was located, near the relatively new settlement of San Angelo. To the west was Devil's River and beyond it the Pecos.

The terrain through which Longarm and Caroline traveled was mostly flat, a plateau that ran all the way from the Panhandle and West Texas almost down to Austin and San Antonio. It was crossed here and there by ranges of rugged hills that might qualify as mountains—if whoever was looking at them had never seen the Rockies.

This was ranching country and not much good for anything else, and it wasn't even really all that good for ranching because of the rocky soil and sparse grass. But there were numerous creeks with sufficient graze along them to support herds of hardy longhorns. Lodestone was probably a supply center for some of the local ranches and owed its existence to them.

The sun was dipping close to the western horizon before Longarm spotted some smoke rising ahead of them. He had begun to think that they might not reach the settlement before darkness fell, which could lead to some further embarrassment if they were forced to spend the night together on the trail.

But the smoke told him they were nearing Lodestone, and sure enough, a few minutes later they topped a rise that let them look down into the valley where the town was located. A good-sized, wooded hill rose west of the settlement, which meant that Lodestone was already in shadow.

Lights burned in the windows of the buildings that lined the single main street. The street ran north and south for three blocks and formed the business district. Residences were located on the cross streets.

Caroline brought the buggy to a halt, and Longarm rode up alongside her before he reined in. She kept her eyes fixed on the scene before her, rather than glancing around at the bodies of the dead outlaws. But her face was tense even though she wasn't looking at the corpses.

"There it is," she said. "Lodestone."

"Yep," Longarm agreed. "I reckon so."

He hadn't asked her what the business was that had brought her here, but he knew from the way she talked that she had never been to Lodestone before. She didn't look like she much wanted to drive down the hill and go there now, either. But as she sat there in the buggy, a determined expression came over her face. She had come this far, and she wasn't going to turn back now.

She forced a smile. "We got here in time for supper."

"Yes, ma'am."

"Shall we go on down there?"

"After you, Miss Thaxter," Longarm said.

Caroline slapped the reins against the horse's back and got the buggy moving again. Longarm followed her down the hill toward the settlement.

They struck a trail at the bottom of the hill. It ran to the southern end of town and turned into the main street when it got there. As Longarm walked his horse along easily, following the buggy, he looked up and down the street, making mental notes of what he saw. That was a habit, too. A good lawman made himself familiar with his surroundings, because there was no telling when such knowledge might be a matter of life and death.

Lodestone appeared to be a typical frontier town, with a large livery stable at the south end of the street and a white-washed, steepled church at the north end. Longarm saw a graveyard behind the church, with tombstones sticking up like grim teeth in the gathering shadows.

Between the stable and the church were numerous businesses, including a hardware store, a saddle shop, a boot-maker, a couple of hotels, several eateries ranging from a nice-looking restaurant to a hole-in-the-wall hash house, a lawyer's office, a doctor's office, an undertaking parlor, a tonsorial parlor and bathhouse, a newspaper, and at least half a dozen saloons.

And a marshal's office and jail, Longarm noted, both housed in a squat, sturdy-looking rock building.

Pointing to a two-story frame building in the next block that had a sign on it reading "LODESTONE HOTEL," he said to Caroline, "That looks like the best place to stay. I'd best stop here at the marshal's office."

She reined in the buggy horse. "Will you be coming over to the hotel later?"

"I expect so. I'll be here for a night or two, anyway, and I'll need a place to stay." Longarm wanted to pay a visit to that bathhouse, too, to get the rest of the grit and dried mud off of him, but he didn't mention that.

Caroline summoned up a smile. "I'll see you later, then," she said. "Perhaps we can have dinner together."

Longarm lifted a hand and touched his fingers to the brim of his hat. "Sounds like a mighty good idea to me, ma'am."

Caroline flicked the reins and drove on. Longarm walked his horse over to the hitchrail in front of the marshal's office, leading the horses with the outlaws' bodies lashed on them. The street wasn't very busy, probably because it was suppertime, but a few people were out and about and Longarm was well aware of the stares he and his charges were getting.

He didn't figure anybody would bother the corpses, so after dismounting, he tied all the reins to the hitchrail and stepped onto the shallow porch in front of the marshal's office. The door was thick and heavy, and instead of windows the building had rifle slits. It looked like a place that would be hard to bust into—or out of.

Longarm didn't know if the marshal was in the office, but he could see light through the rifle slits. He knocked on the door and was answered by a voice calling, "Come in."

He swung the door open and saw a man sitting behind a

22

desk, writing something on a piece of paper in front of him. A marshal's badge pinned to the man's vest gleamed in the lamplight. He had a lantern jaw, weathered skin, and white hair, but he wasn't all that old, just middle-aged. Longarm was a good judge of star packers and figured this one could still handle trouble if it came calling.

The marshal looked up at Longarm and asked, "Something I can do for you, mister?" His blue eyes were mild and friendly.

"You're the local law?"

"That's right. Marshal Artemus Flynn." The marshal pushed his chair back a little and put his pen down, as if he sensed that there might be a problem.

Longarm came on into the office. "I'm Deputy U.S. Marshal Custis Long, out of the Denver office." He took a leather folder out of his shirt pocket and placed it on the desk in front of Flynn. "My badge and bona fides are in there. The identification papers could be a mite smudged, since they got wet in a thunderstorm earlier today. I think you can still read 'em, though."

"Yeah, that cloud blew through here, too. It was a ring-tailed snorter, wasn't it?" Flynn flipped open the folder, looked at the badge and papers it contained, and got to his feet to extend a hand across the desk. "Pleased to meet you, Marshal Long. What can I do for you?"

Longarm shook hands with Flynn, then picked up the folder and put it away. He jerked a thumb over his shoulder. "I've got the bodies of four outlaws out there, tied onto their horses. On the way into town I saw that you've got an undertaker here, so I reckon he'll have some work to do."

Flynn let out a low whistle of surprise. "Four outlaws, you say? And they're all dead?"

"Yep."

"You killed them?"

"They didn't give me much choice in the matter."

"No, I expect not," Flynn said as he came out from behind the desk. He snagged a hat from a nail in the wall. "Let's have a look."

The two lawmen went outside. Flynn left the office door open so that light from inside spilled into the street. Several people were gathered around, obviously curious but keeping their distance from the corpses.

Flynn looked at each body in turn, and Longarm supplied the names that went with them. "They were part of a gang led by Nate Hathaway," he said. "You ever heard of him?"

"Can't say as I have," Flynn said with a shake of his head. "Badman, eh?"

"Him and his bunch have pulled quite a few jobs. I got on their trail after they stuck up an army payroll wagon."

"Do tell. We don't have that kind come through very often. Lodestone's a peaceable town."

"Reckon you could send for the undertaker?" Longarm asked.

"No need." Flynn pointed down the street. "Here he comes now. Somebody must've told him there were four dead men up here in front of my office."

Longarm turned and looked, and saw a wagon being driven along the street by a man in a black suit and a plug hat. When the man brought the wagon to a stop nearby and hopped down from the seat, Longarm saw that he was a wiry little gent with a wizened face. He took his hat off and ran his hand over a bald scalp.

"Looks like a bonanza, Marshal," he said with a grin as he replaced the hat.

"I guess you could say that. Edgar, this is Custis Long. He's a deputy U.S. marshal. Marshal Long, meet Edgar Horne, our undertaker."

Longarm shook hands with Horne, even though he felt an instinctive dislike for the man. He didn't know which was worse undertakers with long, dour faces who were full of doom and gloom, or grinning chucklers like Horne who seemed to find death mighty amusing.

Horne rubbed his hands together in almost gleeful anticipation. A man was riding in the back of the wagon, his legs dangling off the open tailgate, and Horne turned and called to him, "Come and get these bodies, Lonnie. Load 'em up so we can take 'em and get to work on 'em."

"Don't you even want to know who they are?" Longarm asked with a frown.

Horne shook his head. "Doesn't really matter to me, now, does it? My job's the same no matter who they are."

"I'll get all the information from Marshal Long and give it to you later, Edgar," Flynn said. "You'll need their names, anyway, for the markers."

"Yes, I suppose you're right about that."

Lonnie, who was evidently Horne's helper, came up to start loading the corpses in the wagon. He was taller and had broader shoulders than Longarm, who was a pretty big man to start with. Lonnie didn't look too bright; a shock of dark hair fell down over a low forehead. But he was obviously strong, because he lifted Con Haney's body from the horse as soon as Longarm cut it loose, carried the corpse to the back of the wagon, and placed it inside as if Haney didn't weigh much at all. With a shake of his head, Lonnie refused Longarm's offer of help with the bodies.

It didn't take long to transfer them to the back of the wagon. As Lonnie was placing the last of the corpses in there, another man came along the street and walked up to Longarm and Flynn.

"Hello, Doc," Flynn said in greeting to the newcomer. To Longarm, he said, "This is Dr. Hobart Donaldson, sort of our unofficial coroner."

Donaldson was a stocky man with a dark mustache. He shook hands with Longarm and explained, "It's a long way up to the county seat at San Angelo, so when there's a death here I hold an inquest and rule on it. The actual coroner always accepts my verdicts."

Longarm nodded. In a lot of places on the frontier, civilization was sort of sparse, so folks just did the best they could when it came to following official procedures.

25

Donaldson turned to Flynn and asked, "What happened to these men?"

"I don't rightly know," the local lawman replied. "Ought to let Marshal Long tell it, since he brought them in. I assume, though, he had to kill them in the line of duty."

"That's what happened, all right," Longarm said. "They ambushed me, southeast of here, but I was lucky enough to turn the tables on them."

"Four against one, and you're still alive and they're not?" Donaldson nodded solemnly. "That's lucky, all right."

"I was really after their boss," Longarm went on. "Former boss, I should say, since he double-crossed them and took off with the loot from their last job."

"What did you say his name was, again?" Flynn asked.

"Hathaway. Nate Hathaway."

"You heard of him, Doc?"

Donaldson shook his head. "No, I don't believe I have."

The wagon containing the four corpses began to creak off down the street toward the undertaking parlor. Horne handled the reins of the two mules, while big Lonnie perched on the seat beside him.

"What's this fella Hathaway look like, Marshal?" Flynn asked curiously. "You got a reward dodger with his picture on it, or at least a description of him?"

"No reward dodger," Longarm said, "but I can tell you what he looks like because I got a good look at him myself, back over in Junction City, just before the ruckus broke loose with his gang. He's tall, a couple of inches over six feet, with black hair and a sort of high-cheekboned face, so that he looks a little like an Indian even though he's not. Got a scar on his left cheek that runs down under his chin. Looks like he got it in a knife fight, but I ain't sure about that. And he's missing the two littlest fingers on his left hand. I've heard that they got caught in a dally, back when he was doing some cowboying, and got pinched off." Longarm paused and frowned as he realized that both Flynn and Donaldson were now staring at him, eyes wide in surprise. "What is it? What's wrong?"

The marshal and the doctor exchanged a glance, and then Flynn said, "I don't know how to tell you this, Marshal Long, but the man you just described . . . he's here in Lodestone."

Longarm felt anticipation rise. "Where is he? Where can I find him?"

Flynn pointed toward the north end of town and said, "Right up there behind the church . . . in the graveyard."

Chapter 5

"He said his name was Calvin Johnson," Marshal Flynn explained a few minutes later as he, Longarm, and Dr. Donaldson sat in the marshal's office. "He rode into town a couple of days ago."

"He was already a sick man when he got here," Donaldson put in. "Stevens over at the hotel sent a boy to fetch me because some of the other guests were complaining about Johnson's coughing. Or rather, Hathaway's coughing, I guess I should say?"

Longarm slid a cheroot from his pocket. He'd had a supply of them in a tin box in his saddlebags, so they had come through the storm without getting wet.

"So you came to see him?" he asked the doctor as he put the cheroot in his mouth. He left it unlit, but his teeth clamped down on it.

"That's right. I heard him coughing all the way down the hall, before I ever got to his room. Gus went with me to unlock the door. Johnson—Hathaway—whatever his name was, he had the worst case of the grippe that I ever saw. He was just about coughing his guts out. Had a mighty high fever, too. I reckon it was the fever that actually killed him, along about five o'clock the next morning. Nothing I did could get it to come down."

"Was he able to talk to you?"

"A little, but he didn't say much," Donaldson replied. "Just his name, or what he claimed was his name, and that he had been taken sick sudden-like. I didn't have any reason not to believe him."

"No, I know you didn't, Doctor. I don't reckon you did anything wrong. It was good of you to try to take care of him like that."

Donaldson shrugged his beefy shoulders. "I'm a physician. I had to do what I could for him. It just wasn't enough to save him."

As Longarm chewed on the unlit cheroot for a moment, he frowned in thought, tugged on his right earlobe, and then ran his thumbnail down the line of his jaw. "Any chance he could have been poisoned or something like that?"

"Well, I suppose it's possible, but I really don't think it's very likely. I've been a doctor for a long time and seen hundreds of cases of the grippe. I've seen people die from it before, and sometimes it can come on mighty quick, just like Johnson said it did. It's my medical judgment that's what happened here."

"And the coroner's verdict, too," Flynn added. "Got Doc's paperwork right here, all filled out proper-like, and I'll file it with the county the next time I get up to San Angelo. That's the way we handle our records here—file 'em two or three times a year."

"So Hathaway didn't drop any hints that he was an owlhoot on the run from the law and from his former gang, too?"

Flynn said, "I never even saw the man until after he'd passed away, Marshal, so I wouldn't know."

Donaldson shook his head. "Nary a word about that did I hear, Marshal. Sorry."

Longarm felt like cussing but knew it wouldn't do any good. He wasn't upset about Hathaway taking sick and dying. The entire gang was dead now, and good riddance. But

30

there was still that little matter of the missing army payroll . . .

"You said he rode in. Where's his horse now?"

"Down at the livery stable," Flynn said. "It was a pretty good mount, and Ben Monklin, who runs the place, bought it from the town. We'd taken the horse, you know, and the rest of Johnson's gear to help pay for the cost of burying him."

"Liveryman buy the rest of Hathaway's things, too?"

"Just the saddle and tack. Got the rest of it in a box here in my storage room. You're welcome to take a look at it, Marshal, but it doesn't amount to much."

Longarm got to his feet. "Thanks. I'd like to see it."

Flynn stood as well. "Sure. Storeroom's back here behind the cell block. Come with me."

Donaldson got up and said, "Reckon I'll go on back home if you don't need me for anything else, Marshal. Either of you marshals."

Longarm shook his head. "Nope. Thanks, Doc."

"Yeah, thanks, Doc," Flynn added. Then he led Longarm down a short hall past two iron-barred cells, one on either side. He unlocked a narrow door that opened into a cluttered storage room.

Flynn struck a match and lit a lamp. By its flickering light, Longarm poked through a wooden box that contained some clothes, a hat, a pair of saddlebags, and a coiled shell belt with a holstered Colt attached to it. Inside the saddlebags he found some crumpled bills, a few coins, a tobacco pouch, a small cardboard box half-full of .44–40 cartridges, and several letters that were creased, worn, and faded from much handling.

As Longarm looked at the letters, Flynn said, "You know, I see now that those were written to somebody named Nate, but I never noticed that before. To tell you the truth, I didn't look at them that close. Didn't seem right to be intruding into a dead man's life. I glanced at them to check for an address maybe, to see if there was anybody I needed to notify about what happened to him, but when I saw there were no envelopes, and no address on any of the letters, I just stuck 'em back in the saddlebag."

"Reckon I probably would've done the same thing," Longarm said. "This is all he had?"

"That's it, except for his horse and that Winchester rifle leaning in the corner over there. Wasn't room for it in the box."

Longarm nodded slowly. He didn't like to admit it to himself, but he knew he had reached a literal dead end. Hathaway must have cached that army payroll money somewhere before riding into Lodestone. Knowing that he was sick, he could have hidden the money and planned to come back for it after he had recuperated.

Only he hadn't recuperated, and now there was no way of knowing what he had done with the loot. Longarm couldn't even try to backtrack him, because the heavy rain earlier in the day would have washed out any prints.

Frustration gnawed at Longarm's guts. He hated to leave a job half-done. He would have to go back to Denver and report to Billy Vail that Hathaway and the other outlaws were dead, but the payroll was probably gone forever. Vail would understand that under the circumstances, there wasn't anything else Longarm could do.

But that didn't mean Longarm had to be satisfied with the outcome of this case. No, sir.

As he and Flynn went back into the office, Longarm said, "Reckon I ought to take a look at Hathaway's grave, just so I can say I checked it out."

"Sure thing. Want to go up to the graveyard right now?"

Longarm shook his head. "No, tomorrow will do just fine. I'll go over to the hotel and get a room and something to eat."

He didn't say anything about meeting Caroline Thaxter for dinner. It was probably too late for that, anyway. Stopping at Flynn's office had taken him longer than he'd expected, and he wouldn't be surprised if Caroline had already eaten and maybe even turned in for the night.

Flynn held out his hand. "Well, I'll see you in the morning then, Marshal. If there's anything you need between now and then, just let me know. I'll be here. I've got a cabin on Hickory Street, but I generally sleep in one of the cells."

"You don't have a night deputy?" Longarm asked as he shook hands.

Flynn smiled. "Don't need one. Like I said, Lodestone's a peaceable town."

Longarm went out and got his horse and the outlaws' mounts and led all the animals down the street to the livery stable. Ben Monklin would probably wind up with the gang's horses, too. It seemed fitting somehow.

When Longarm had turned all the horses over to the liveryman, he walked up the street to the Lodestone Hotel. As he went into the lobby, he glanced to his left through an arched entrance into the dining room, hoping to see Caroline Thaxter even though he didn't really expect to.

He saw her, all right. He also saw what looked like trouble.

Caroline sat at one of the tables in the dining room. She had taken off her hat and the jacket from her traveling outfit. She wore a white, frilly blouse that looked nice on her, and her auburn hair gleamed redly in the lamplight. Longarm thought she would have looked mighty fetching if not for the anxious, almost frightened expression on her face.

That expression was because of the young man standing beside the table, grinning down at her. He wore range clothes, but they were clean and pressed. The Stetson that was cuffed back on curly fair hair was creamy and had never known the stain of mud or rain or sweat. Longarm figured the man had never done any real cowboying in his life.

The ivory grips of the revolver on the man's hip had seen considerable use, though.

"C'mon, honey," the man was saying as Longarm came through the entrance into the hotel dining room. "Why don't you come on down to the saloon with me and have a drink?"

"No, thank you," Caroline said in a tight voice. "I'm not in the habit of frequenting saloons."

"No, I reckon a lady like you wouldn't be. How about I go get a bottle then, and we'll go up to your room and drink it?"

"That would be even more improper."

"No, no, there wouldn't be nothin' improper about it." Nonchalantly, the man leaned closer to Caroline and rested his left hand on the table. "I just like to see that everybody who comes to Lodestone gets a nice, friendly welcome."

"What about me?" Longarm asked coldly as he came up behind the man. "Do I get a nice, friendly welcome, old son?"

The man straightened and looked over his shoulder. At the same time, Caroline raised her eyes to Longarm and gazed at him in obvious relief.

"I wasn't talkin' to you, mister," the man said with an annoyed frown. "Why don't you move along and leave me and the lady to our business?"

Longarm said, "Because you ain't got no business with her, and it's a mite insulting for you to imply that you do."

The man turned so that he was facing Longarm. He hooked his thumbs in his gunbelt. "I'll imply anything I damned well please, you son of a bitch, and if you don't go on and leave me alone, I'll back it up, too."

A faint, humorless smile touched Longarm's mouth. "That's an apple you don't want to be takin' a bite out of, old son."

The man's face darkened with anger. "Do you know who I am?"

"We ain't been introduced, but I generally recognize a jackass when I see one."

There were no other hotel guests in the room, only a

34

waitress in a white apron. In a hurry, she ducked through a door at the back of the room, and Longarm figured she was going to fetch the cook or maybe the owner of the hotel.

Caroline said shakily, "Gentlemen, please—"

"Shut up," the man snapped. "Your friend here started this, and now he can damn well take what's comin' to him. And when I'm done with that . . . so can you." The leer came back to his face. "You'll enjoy it. Wait and see."

He was trying to goad Longarm into drawing, figuring that he wouldn't have any trouble killing this stranger. Longarm had done a little goading himself with that jackass comment. As a result, the air in the dining room was thick with tension.

The door in the back of the room opened quickly, and a middle-aged man in a suit came into the dining room. "Riley, please!" he said. "We don't need any trouble—"

"Don't tell me what I need, Stevens," the man called Riley said without looking around. "As for you, you need to go—"

What he told Stevens to do next was a physical impossibility, and obscene to boot. Caroline paled at the language.

"Well, mister?" Riley went on to Longarm. "You gonna draw, or am I gonna have to shoot you down in cold blood?"

Longarm sighed. "Are you bound and determined to do that?"

Riley's sneer, and the way his hand now hovered over the butt of the ivory-handled Colt, said that he was.

"Then start the ball, old son," Longarm said softly, and Riley's hand flashed down to his gun.

Chapter 6

The kid was fast; Longarm had to give him that. Not as fast as he thought he was, though, and not nearly fast enough.

Longarm's fist came up and shot across the space between them to slam into Riley's mouth. The punch landed before the fancy gun was even halfway out of its holster. Riley went backward about four feet before he tripped over an empty chair and crashed down on top of a table with its red-checked tablecloth. The tabletop cracked and the legs gave way under the sudden weight. The table collapsed, and Riley sprawled on the floor amid the wreckage, stunned.

"Oh, my goodness," Caroline breathed. Stevens, the hotel owner, had a look of shock on his face, and so did the waitress, who peeped out from behind him.

Longarm packed a pretty powerful punch to start with, and he had channeled all of his considerable annoyance and frustration with the way the day had gone into that single blow. It had landed cleanly, and he wasn't surprised with the result. He didn't really expect Riley to get up.

But that was what happened. With a bloody mouth and lips already so swollen that his cursing was pretty much indecipherable, Riley pushed himself off the floor, grabbed one of the broken chair legs, and rushed at Longarm, swinging the makeshift club.

Obviously, gunplay wouldn't be enough to settle this now. Riley wanted to beat Longarm to death.

Longarm was equally determined to prevent that, so he twisted aside, let the chair leg whip harmlessly through the space where his head had been, and stuck a booted foot between Riley's ankles. Already off-balance from the missed blow, Riley careened out of control. Longarm hammered a punch into the small of his back as the young man went past.

Riley went down again, face first this time. The chair leg clattered away from him. "Stay down," Longarm warned him.

The warning didn't do any good. Riley clambered up again. He was young, strong, and reasonably quick. He had probably won every fight he'd had in his life. He couldn't understand why he wasn't winning this one. Still grunting incoherent curses through his battered lips, he charged at Longarm again.

He was a little more cautious this time, however, and some of his natural skill at brawling began to assert itself. He threw a lot of punches, but they weren't wild ones. Longarm had to work to block them. Riley kept him so busy warding off blows that he didn't have a chance to throw any punches of his own.

Riley was good enough to get a hard right cross past Longarm's guard. The young man's fist caught Longarm on the jaw and rocked him back a step. That must have sent Riley's confidence soaring, because he immediately abandoned what he had been doing and bulled in again, ready to pound his opponent to death with his bare hands.

He ran straight into a short, jabbing left that stopped him in his tracks and set him up for the looping right that exploded on his jaw. This time when Riley went down in a crumpled heap on the floor, it was apparent to everyone in the room that he wasn't going to be getting up again any time soon.

Ruefully, Longarm rubbed his jaw where Riley had tagged him. The kid never should have landed even that one punch. Longarm wondered if he was slowing down, getting old.

"My God!" Caroline said. "I never saw anything like that."

Stevens bustled over, an angry look on his face. "Did you have to thrash him like that?" he demanded as he glared at Longarm.

"Well, I could have shot him," Longarm said, "but then you'd have had to mop all that blood off the floor. Sorry about your table, though. I recko'n I'll pay for the damages, although by all rights that fella on the floor ought to."

"Do you know who he is?" Stevens asked shakily.

"The way he acted before and the way you're acting now, I'd say he's the big skookum he-wolf around here . . . or at least he thinks he is."

A footstep sounded at the entrance to the dining room, and a familiar voice said, "He's Riley Bascomb. His father is the mayor of Lodestone."

Longarm looked around to see Marshal Artemus Flynn standing there, a shotgun tucked under his arm. Longarm rubbed his jaw again and said, "I reckon that'd make his pa your boss, then, wouldn't it, Marshal?"

"You could say that," Flynn agreed dryly. "When somebody came running over to my office and said a madman was tearing up the dining room of the Lodestone Hotel, I never figured it would be you, Marshal."

Stevens stared at Longarm and repeated, "Marshal?"

Flynn came on into the dining room. "That's right, Milt. This here is Deputy U.S. Marshal Custis Long."

"So you're going to take his side in this?" Stevens asked.

"Well, over and above the fact that Marshal Long is a

fellow lawman, I happen to know from experience that Riley Bascomb is a hotheaded young fool who gets into trouble on a regular basis. How many fistfights and shooting scrapes has Riley been in over the past couple of years?"

"Riley's, uh, a high-spirited young fella," Stevens said.

Caroline spoke up, saying to Flynn, "Are you the town marshal, sir?"

Flynn touched a finger to the brim of his hat. "Yes, ma'am, I am. Marshal Artemus Flynn, at your service."

"I can testify that this altercation wasn't Marshal Long's fault." She pointed at Riley Bascomb. "This man was trying to force his attentions on me, and he was very rude and insulting about it. Marshal Long was simply defending me."

Flynn nodded slowly. "Yes, ma'am, when I walked in and saw a beautiful woman sitting here, I figured it must've been something like that. On top of his other qualities, Riley considers himself to be God's gift to women."

Longarm had seen plenty of young bucks like Riley Bascomb. Riley thought that because his father was the mayor and probably the richest man in town as well, he could do whatever he damned well pleased and get away with it. He would be right about that, too—most of the time.

But not tonight.

"Are you going to arrest me, Marshal?" Longarm asked Flynn.

"Nope." Flynn gestured toward the broken table. "That get busted in the fracas, Milt?"

"Yeah," Stevens replied.

"I'm sure Hugh will be glad to pay for the damages. I'll tell him about it tomorrow and square things with him."

Stevens looked relieved. "That's mighty decent of you, Artemus. Thank you."

"Just part of my job," Flynn said. "Making sure things go as smooth and peaceful as possible in Lodestone." He turned back to Longarm. "You planning to stay here, Marshal?"

"I had planned on it. I reckon I can find a room in one of the other hotels, though, if need be."

"Oh, I'm sure that won't be the case. You don't mind if Marshal Long stays here, do you, Milt?"

"Glad to have you, Marshal," Stevens said, a slightly surly tone to his voice. Longarm chose to ignore it.

Flynn smiled at Caroline. "And, ma'am, you are . . . ?"

"Miss Caroline Thaxter. Marshal Long and I are traveling together."

"Is that so." Flynn's carefully neutral voice made sure there was no offense attached to the words. He touched the brim of his hat again and went on, "I'm very pleased to meet you, Miss Thaxter."

"Are you going to lock up Riley?" Longarm asked.

"No need for that. I'll haul him out of here and dunk his head in the horse trough a couple of times. Then I'll send him back to his pa's house. I think he'll stay out of trouble for a while, at least as long as you're here in town, Marshal. I'll see to it."

"All right." Longarm wasn't going to argue with Flynn's decision. The local lawman knew the situation around here better than he did. Flynn didn't act like he was the least bit buffaloed by the fact that Riley's father was the mayor, but on the other hand, he was going to handle things with as much discretion as he could. Longarm couldn't fault him for that.

Flynn set his shotgun on one of the tables and then got Riley to his feet. With an arm around the young man's waist, he picked up the greener and steered Riley out of the dining room, through the lobby, and out of the hotel.

"You want some supper, Marshal?" Stevens asked, again with an air of surliness. "Our serving hours are over, but there's still some food on the stove."

Longarm wasn't going to let the man's attitude bother him. "I'd like that," he said. "I'm much obliged."

41

Stevens turned and said to the waitress, "Bring Marshal Long some supper, Hannah. I'll get your room key, Marshal."

"You want me to sign the book?"

"You can do that later."

Longarm sat down with Caroline. She had the remains of a meal on a plate in front of her, and half a cup of coffee that had gone cold. Longarm would ask Hannah to freshen it up when she came back.

"Thank you, Marshal," Caroline said quietly when they were alone.

"Why don't you call me Custis?" Longarm suggested.

Caroline smiled. "Yes, since you've risked life and limb defending my honor, I suppose I should do that."

"It wasn't all that much of a risk," Longarm said with a smile. "Riley Bascomb may be a big fish in this pond, but I've dealt with a whole heap worse in my time."

"I'm sure you have. Have you brought in a lot of notorious desperadoes?"

"My share," Longarm admitted. "I've been a star packer for Uncle Sam for a while, and it's been a pretty busy time."

"Are all your days as hectic as this one?"

Longarm shook his head. "No, a lot of days I don't kill anybody at all."

Caroline smiled, but she shivered a little, too. "I don't know whether to be impressed by you, Custis, or afraid of you."

"You don't have anything to be afraid of where I'm concerned," Longarm told her.

"Yes," she said. "I believe that. I'm very glad we met, and not just because you were here to save me from that awful Riley Bascomb."

"I'm glad, too," Longarm said.

Stevens came into the dining room and laid a room key on the table in front of Longarm. "Room eight," he said. "Up the stairs, third door on the right."

"Much obliged," Longarm told him with a nod.

Stevens went back to the lobby. Caroline reached across the table and put a fingertip on the room key. "Room eight," she said. "I'm in Room seven. That's right across the hall. I'm glad you'll be so close to me, Custis."

Longarm saw the sparkle in her green eyes as she spoke, and suddenly he was mighty glad they were going to be so close, too.

Chapter 7

For the next half hour, Longarm sat and talked with Caroline Thaxter while he ate his supper and drank a couple of cups of coffee. Caroline lingered at the table over coffee, obviously enjoying the time she spent with Longarm. By the time they finished eating, a comfortable air existed between them, as if they were old friends.

"What are your plans for the rest of the evening, Custis?" she asked when he pushed his plate away.

"There's a barbershop and bathhouse down the street," Longarm said. "I thought I might see if it's still open. If it is, I intend to spruce up a mite. Rolling around in the mud and then trying to wash off in a muddy creek don't leave a man feeling very clean."

"No, I expect it doesn't. Will I see you later?"

"I reckon that depends. Were you planning to go upstairs and turn in?"

"I might go ahead and get ready for bed," Caroline said with a smile, "but I'm not really sleepy. Why don't you knock on my door when you get back and see if I'm still awake?"

"I'll do that," Longarm promised with a smile of his own.

He was still smiling a few minutes later when he walked into Hukill's Tonsorial Parlor and asked if he could still get

45

a hot bath. The barber, a middle-aged man with the stub of a fat cigar clenched between his teeth, got up from the barber chair where he'd been sitting and reading the paper.

"I was just about to close up for the night, mister," he said, "but there's still some hot water in the pot in back. If you don't mind fixin' the bath yourself, you're welcome to it. Four bits for the water and the use of the tub."

"Sounds fine. What about a shave?"

The barber grinned around the cigar. "You'll have to do that yourself, too. I'm goin' home. Just leave the money there on the shelf when you're done."

"You want me to lock up when I leave?"

"No need," the barber said. "Lodestone is a peaceable town."

"Yeah, that's what everybody keeps telling me," Longarm said dryly as he thought about the run-in he'd had with Riley Bascomb. Riley hadn't been peaceable at all— but maybe he was the exception that proved the rule.

Longarm headed out back to the bathhouse, which was connected to the barbershop by a covered walk. He found a galvanized tin tub, several buckets, and a large black cast-iron pot sitting on a stove. The fire was out, but it hadn't been for long. Wisps of steam still rose from the water in the pot. Longarm used one of the buckets to fill the tub, then started stripping his clothes off.

A couple of chairs were in the room as well. He put them beside the tub, coiled his gunbelt on one and draped his clothes over the other. When he was naked, he stepped into the tub and sank down gratefully into the water.

The hot water felt mighty good. He reached over to his clothes, found a cheroot and a lucifer, and lit the thin cigar. Leaning back in the tub, Longarm closed his eyes, puffed on the cheroot, and felt tense, sore muscles begin to unkink and relax.

He sat there for a while, smoking and soaking, before he reached down to the floor beside the tub and picked up a brush and a hunk of soap. As pleasant as this was, Caroline was waiting for him, and the last thing he wanted was for her to doze off before he got there.

Longarm soaped himself up and used the brush to scrub off all the mud that had dried on him in various places. He scrubbed until his skin glowed pink. Finally feeling clean again, he stood up in the tub and reached for a towel that hung over a nearby rack.

A bullet tore through the wall as a gun blasted just outside the bathhouse. With a clang of metal, the slug struck the rack holding the towel and toppled it. Another bullet punched through the wall and whipped past Longarm's head, so close to his ear that he heard the wind-rip of its passage.

He dropped swiftly into a crouch, hunkering down inside the tin bathtub. He didn't know if the tub would stop a bullet or not—probably not—but it was the closest thing to some cover he was going to find in here. His hand shot out and closed around the butt of the Colt as another bullet sang past, too close for comfort.

Longarm took a deep breath and ducked under the soapy water. He felt the vibration as a slug hit the tub. The hand holding the revolver was still above the water, so he triggered twice in the general direction of whoever was trying to kill him. At this range, the handgun rounds would penetrate the thin walls of the bathhouse just as well as the rifle bullets would.

As he became aware that the water level in the tub was dropping, Longarm realized that the shot must have holed the tin. That was how close he had come to dying—again. This had been a dangerous day.

But the shooting seemed to have stopped. Cautiously, he poked his head up as water continued to gurgle out through the bullet holes in the tub. The slug had gone all the way through, from one side to the other.

Longarm blinked rapidly and shoved his wet hair back from his eyes. He surged up, rolled out of the tub, and sprawled flat on his belly on the floor, making himself as small a target as possible if the bushwhacker tried again.

Hurrying footsteps sounded outside, and a figured appeared in the doorway. Longarm held off on the trigger as he recognized Marshal Artemus Flynn. The local lawman carried a shotgun and was obviously responding to the shots.

Flynn stopped short and his eyes widened as he spotted Longarm's nude figure lying on the floor. "Good Lord, Marshal!" he exploded. "Are you all right?"

Longarm ignored the question and asked one of his own. "Did you see somebody running off from here just now?"

"No, I didn't. What was all that shooting about?"

"Somebody tried to kill me. Take a look at the wall over there. You'll see the holes where the bullets came through."

Flynn stepped closer to the wall, studied it for a moment, and nodded. "Those are bullet holes, sure enough. Got any idea who it was?"

"Unless he was still with you," Longarm said, "I'd take a good long look at Riley Bascomb."

A grim expression came over Flynn's weathered face. "I sent Riley home more'n half an hour ago, after I gave him that water trough dunkin' and a good talking to."

"Then he had plenty of time to get a rifle and come back here to try to kill me."

"How'd he know you were here?" Flynn asked.

"Maybe he saw me when I left the hotel and followed me down here."

"Maybe." Flynn grimaced. "When I ask him about this, though, he's going to deny it up one way and down the other. And there probably won't be any way for me to prove that he's lying . . . if he is."

"I haven't had any problems with anybody else in Lodestone," Longarm pointed out. "He's the only one with a reason to try to ventilate me. I reckon his pride was pretty injured by that whipping I gave him."

"He wasn't happy, I can tell you that." Flynn shook his head. "I wouldn't have thought that Riley would try to murder you, though."

"You said he'd been in shooting scrapes before." Longarm set the gun aside and picked up the towel from the floor. After shaking any dirt off of it, he began to dry himself.

"Riley's had some gunfights," Flynn admitted. "And I know he prodded the other fellas into drawing. But they always drew first. The fights were fair, nothing I could do about them."

"Sometimes when a man gets killing in his blood, it gets easier and easier for him as he goes along."

"I'll have a talk with him, and with his pa, too," Flynn promised. "But like I said, I probably won't be able to prove anything."

Longarm knew that the local lawman was right. If Riley Bascomb was the one who had taken those shots at him—and Longarm was convinced that he was—then he might well get away with it.

But there would be another time. Longarm was convinced of that, too. Riley wasn't the sort who would give up on trying to even the score.

"I guess you're headed back to the hotel from here?" Flynn asked as Longarm got dressed.

"That's right."

"I'll walk along with you. Less chance of anything happening that way."

They walked out through the barbershop. Longarm left some extra money on the shelf. The barber would have to fix those bullet holes in the wall and replace that tub. Longarm knew that Henry, Billy Vail's clerk up in Denver, would object to seeing those expenses on the official report, but he would just have to put up with it. Nobody else was going to cover those damages.

"You know, since I've been in Lodestone, I've been in a fight and been shot at," Longarm mused as he and Flynn walked up the street. "I'm starting to think this ain't such a peaceful place after all."

Flynn sighed. "Maybe you're right. The world's changing, and not for the better. Why, it's only been a week or so since I had to shoot and kill a robber who was trying to break into a store one night while I was making my rounds."

Longarm glanced over at him. "Is that so?"

The local lawman nodded and said, "Yeah. It had been quite a while since I'd had to draw my gun. Now . . . well, I just don't know what's going to happen next." He chuckled but didn't sound very amused. "If it wasn't for that, I'd be tempted to say that *you're* a jinx, Marshal. Maybe you brought the trouble to Lodestone with you."

Longarm frowned. He hadn't thought of that. It was true that violence and sudden death were his saddle partners, and it had been that way for a long time. But that was just the nature of the business he was in. A man who dealt with lawbreakers all the time couldn't avoid trouble.

That was evidently Marshal Flynn's goal, though, and Longarm couldn't blame him for that.

They reached the hotel, and Flynn said again, "I'll have that talk with Riley Bascomb and the mayor in the morning. Stop by the office, if you're still in town, and I'll fill you in on what they have to say."

"Sure," Longarm said, not holding out much hope that Flynn's conversation with the Bascombs would yield any positive results. Riley would just deny everything, and his father would probably believe him.

Longarm went into the hotel. Stevens was behind the desk. He didn't look any too pleased to see Longarm. The big lawman ignored him and crossed the lobby to the stairs.

He didn't go to his own room but stopped in front of the door to room seven instead. With a knuckle, he rapped quietly on the door. He heard a soft footstep on the other side, and Caroline asked, "Custis?"

"That's right," he told her.

The knob turned and the door eased open. "Come in," she said, "and close the door behind you."

She was already standing by the bed by the time Longarm was completely in the room and had eased the door shut. She turned to face him, and Longarm was glad that he had learned patience over the years.

That old saying about how good things came to him who waited was sure as blazes true in this case.

Chapter 8

Caroline wore a gauzy, pale green nightdress that was thin enough to reveal the sleek lines of her body. She had let down her hair so that it fell around her shoulders in auburn waves. In the dim light from the lamp on the bedside table, she was as lovely a woman as Longarm had seen in quite some time.

She didn't seem to mind, either, that he was letting his eyes play boldly over her face and form. Her lips curved in a faint smile as Longarm studied the proud thrust of her creamy breasts with their coral tips. His gaze slid down over her belly to the sensuous swell of her hips and the triangle of dark red hair between her legs.

"You're not going to just stand there all night, are you, Custis?" she asked softly.

"Not hardly," Longarm replied. He moved across the room toward her, and she came eagerly into his arms.

Their mouths met in a hot, searching kiss. His arms tightened around her, drawing her against him until her body was molded to his. The soft warmth of her flesh, combined with the hot sweetness of her mouth, sent a pulse of desire throbbing through him.

His manhood had already started to harden before he took her in his embrace. After a moment of kissing and holding her, it was like a bar of iron. She moaned deep in her throat as she ground her belly against his shaft.

He slid one hand down her back to explore the curves of her hips. The other hand moved between them and found the soft mound of her right breast. As he cupped it through the thin fabric, he felt the nipple hardening against his palm.

Caroline's lips parted in invitation. Longarm's tongue delved into the hot, wet cavern of her mouth and met her tongue. They dueled there, circling and thrusting, for long moments. Finally, they broke the kiss. Caroline gasped for breath. Her chest heaved, making her breasts move tantalizingly against Longarm's broad chest.

"I knew it," she said. "I knew as soon as I saw you that I wanted you, Custis."

"Well, considering that I was buck naked at the time, I'm mighty glad that was your reaction," he said. "You might've screamed and run the other way."

"As you said," she purred, "not hardly."

She moved out of his arms and stepped back enough so that she could reach his belt buckle and the buttons of his trousers. Her fingers deftly unfastened them. Longarm peeled his shirt up and over his head and tossed it onto a chair as Caroline lowered his trousers. As she pulled the long underwear bottoms down, Longarm's hard shaft sprang free. It jutted out proudly from the thick mat of dark hair on his groin.

Caroline's knees seemed to get a little weak as she gazed at the long, thick pole of male flesh. She sat down on the edge of the bed behind her. That put her wide green eyes on the same level as Longarm's member. She reached up with both hands and tried to close them around it.

"My God," she said in awe as her fingers failed to quite meet. "I knew you were big, but I hadn't seen it hard yet." She stroked her palms along the shaft and leaned forward to run her tongue around the crown. Then, opening her mouth as far as she could, she closed her lips around the head and began to suck gently.

Longarm's jaw tightened as her oral caress sent waves of pleasure through him. He stroked her thick, auburn hair as she bent to her task. She spoke French exceedingly well, and he enjoyed every second of it. After a while she insinuated a hand between his legs and cupped his heavy balls in her palm. His hips twitched, but he suppressed the impulse to thrust himself deeper into her mouth. He didn't want to choke her.

She seemed to sense when she had brought him to the brink, because she drew back. With a quick movement, she pulled the nightdress off. As she sprawled on her back, her legs parted, revealing the wet opening of her sex. Droplets of feminine dew sparkled here and there among the fine-spun hair.

"My turn," she said breathlessly.

Longarm was glad to oblige, but he didn't get in any hurry about it. Instead he sat down on the chair where he had thrown his shirt and pulled his boots and socks off. Then he slid his legs out of the trousers and long underwear. When he stood up, he was as naked as Caroline was. Then and only then did he move onto the bed.

Her breasts rose and fell rapidly. Little shivers ran through the soft, pale flesh of her stomach. Her hands stole between her legs and rubbed at the damp folds. "Custis," she said, desperation edging into her voice.

Longarm didn't make her wait any longer. He leaned over between her widespread thighs and began using his lips and tongue on her with the same sort of skill she had applied to him. His thumbs parted the folds so that his tongue could spear deeply into her. Her hips bucked up off the bed, and she wrapped her legs around his head, the inside of her thighs pressing hard against his ears.

He hoped she wasn't the sort of gal who got carried away and started screaming. The owner of this hotel was already peeved enough about the fracas with Riley Bascomb. He wouldn't want the rest of his guests disturbed.

Longarm didn't spare much thought for that possibility, however. He was too busy keeping up with Caroline. She urged him on for long minutes, and she cried out softly in disappointment when he finally lifted his head. The next second, though, he had moved between her legs and brought the head of his shaft to her drenched opening. So she didn't have very long to be disappointed.

She was so wet that he entered her with no trouble, surging forward until most of his manhood was buried inside her. Caroline clutched at him, twining her arms around his neck and locking her ankles together above his thrusting hips.

Longarm paced himself, falling into the steady, universal rhythm that lifted both of them higher and higher toward the peak of their lovemaking. Caroline met him thrust for thrust, every bit as eager and avid as he was. As aroused as both of them were, it was no surprise that in a matter of mere moments they were nearing culmination.

As Longarm felt his climax about to break, he drove forward until he was sheathed completely inside her, as deep as he could go. He stayed there instead of drawing back for another stroke, and his juices burst from him in a senses-shattering explosion of white heat.

At the same time Caroline spasmed wildly, shaken by her own climax. She shook and shuddered and held him tighter than ever. Longarm emptied himself inside her. Only when he was completely drained and had to gasp for air did he realize that he had been holding his breath.

His muscles were left limp by the intensity of their shared experience. He didn't want to crush Caroline with his weight, though, so after a few seconds he summoned up the strength and the willpower to roll off of her. He sprawled on his back beside her, and she turned so that she was snuggled up against him, in the curve of his arm. Both of them were covered in a fine sheen of sweat. She reached down and gently cupped a hand around his softening organ.

"I . . . I was right," she managed to say. "I knew it would be good between us as soon as I saw you, Custis."

"It was . . . mighty fine . . . all right," Longarm said as he tried to catch his breath. His pulse galloped. He stroked Caroline's flank, relishing the feel of her soft, smooth skin.

They lay there, quiet for the most part, as they recovered. Caroline kissed Longarm's shoulder and ran her fingers through the carpet of brown hair on his chest. After a while she raised herself on an elbow and frowned down at him.

"What's wrong?" he asked.

"Custis, you have scars all over you! I noticed some of them out there at the creek when you were, well, you know, undressed, but I didn't realize there were quite so many of them. Where did they all come from?"

"Oh, bullets, knives, the occasional tomahawk or Indian lance, a run-in or two with bears and mountain lions . . ."

She laughed. "You sound like a character from some sort of dime novel, one of those made-up frontiersmen who are always getting into trouble."

"Well, I *am* a lawman. A fella in my line of work tends to run into a lot of different scrapes and ruckuses."

Caroline grew more serious. "You should take better care of yourself. I'd hate to think of anything terrible happening to you."

"I'll be careful," Longarm promised solemnly.

She laughed. "I doubt that. I can tell that you're a wild man, Custis Long. It's just your nature."

"Well . . . maybe."

She rested her head on his shoulder again and sighed. A few minutes of companionable silence went by before Caroline said, "Custis, there's something I really need to tell you, something you need to know about me."

"Don't go trying to tell me that you ain't a gal, because I know better."

She smiled and said, "No, I'm a hundred percent woman, and a very satisfied woman, at that." She paused, then went on, "It has to do with the reason I came to Lodestone in the first place. Aren't you curious about that?"

Even though he was lying down, Longarm managed to shrug. "Didn't figure it was really any of my business, so I didn't pry. I'll admit I was a mite curious, though, about a beautiful woman like you traveling by herself. You don't see that too often out here on the frontier."

"I was traveling by myself because I don't have any family left except for my father, and he's the reason I'm here."

"He lives in Lodestone?" Longarm asked, a little surprised.

Caroline shook her head. "No, but I've been looking for him for a long time, and I heard a rumor that he was heading in this direction. I thought I might catch up to him here."

"You want me to help you look for him? The case that brought me here is over, but I might be able to stay around for a day or two—"

"No, I don't think that would be a good idea."

Longarm heard the strain in her voice. "Why not?" he asked.

Caroline took a deep breath and said, "Because you see, Custis, my father is a wanted man. An outlaw."

Chapter 9

Longarm sat up. "An outlaw?" he repeated. Somehow it almost didn't seem possible that a gal as nice as Caroline could have an owlhoot for a father.

But as the old saying went, you couldn't pick your relatives, and he recalled other people he had met who were the offspring of lawbreakers. A few of them had been among the finest people on the face of the earth.

"I . . . I didn't know whether to tell you or not," Caroline went on, "what with you being a lawman and all."

"If your pa ain't wanted on federal warrants, I wouldn't have any jurisdiction where he's concerned," he pointed out.

"I don't know about that. I haven't seen him for several years. And for years before that, he was sort of . . . in and out of my life. He came to see my mother and me sometimes, but we were never close. Before my mother died, she asked me to promise that I would find him and tell him what happened to her."

"What did happen to her?" Longarm asked. "That is, if you're sure you want to talk about this."

Caroline sat up, too, and said, "I think I need to talk about it. That's why I brought it up. I can tell that you're not the sort of man who'd look down on me just because of the things my father did."

"Of course not," Longarm said, and felt a little ashamed because he'd had to remind himself not to do that very thing.

Caroline was beautiful as ever in the lamplight, with her hair tousled from lovemaking, but Longarm put those thoughts aside as she began to explain about the circumstances that had brought her to Lodestone.

"My mother and I lived in Omaha, and that's where my father came to visit us. I'm sure he was around some when I was an infant, but I don't remember ever seeing him until I was four or five years old. I was so impressed with him. He was tall and wore a big hat and chaps, and he carried a gun and smelled like . . . like I didn't know what. I know now, of course, that it was whiskey and tobacco and horses he smelled like, but I didn't then. You'd think a little girl wouldn't care for that, but . . . he was my father."

Longarm nodded. "I reckon I understand."

"But then he'd leave, and I cried because he was gone, and that went on for years, until I stopped crying when he left and got mad at him instead. I could see how much his comings and goings hurt my mother, and I knew how much they hurt me."

"Some fellas want to do the right thing," Longarm said slowly. "It's just that they ain't overly sure of what the right thing is."

"Despite everything he did, I don't think my father was truly an evil man. Since I got older, I've tried to find out more about him. As far as I know, he never killed anyone in any of his robberies. He just stole money, mostly from trains and banks."

"A lot of men have done that. Makes 'em outlaws, not monsters."

Caroline nodded. "I began to understand that. Then my mother got sick and died, but like I said, she made me promise that I'd find my father. I think that more than anything else, she wanted the two of us to see each other again.

She didn't want there to be any bad blood between us." She shrugged. "So I've been looking for him for the past couple of years. I tracked down some men who knew him, and one of them said he thought my father was headed in this direction. He specifically mentioned Lodestone."

"These fellas you talked to . . . they were outlaws, too?"

"Well, yes, I suppose so." Caroline frowned. "Do you think it was a lie?"

"Could be they didn't trust you and didn't want you to find your pa," Longarm said. "Maybe he told them that if anybody came looking for him, to put them on the wrong trail."

Caroline looked stricken. "Oh, my God, you're right, Custis. That could be exactly what happened."

Longarm slipped an arm around her shoulders and drew her against him to comfort her. "It's still possible that the hombre told you the truth," he said. "What you need to do is ask around town and find out if anybody here has seen your pa. I'll even help you if you want."

She turned her head to look up at him. "You'd do that for me, Custis?"

"Why, sure," he answered without hesitation. "Like I told you, the case that brought me here is over. The fella I was looking for is dead." Quickly, he sketched in the details of his pursuit of Nate Hathaway and what he had learned about Hathaway's death from Marshal Flynn and Dr. Donaldson.

"So it looks like I won't be able to recover that stolen army payroll," he concluded, "but with Hathaway and all the other members of his gang dead, there's nothing else I can do."

"But don't you have to get back to Denver? Isn't that where you said your office is?"

"As soon as I wire my boss, Billy Vail, about what happened, then yeah, he'll expect me to start home so that he can give me some other chore." Longarm smiled. "But there ain't no telegraph office in Lodestone. You're the one who told me that, remember?"

"Then if you stayed for a little while to help me . . ."

"Nobody would ever know the difference," Longarm said.

"I would," Caroline said softly. "And I'd appreciate it so much, Custis." As she snuggled closer in his arms, she reached down and stroked his manhood, which had grown semi-erect again purely from the fact that he was sitting there with a nude, beautiful woman beside him. As his shaft hardened once more into a full erection under her touch, she went on, "In fact, I'd like to show you just how much I appreciate your help." She leaned over and took him into her mouth.

Longarm didn't argue with her. He would have helped her anyway, no matter what she did, but since she was feeling grateful, he thought it would be rude to tell her to stop what she was doing.

Especially when it felt so damned good . . .

Longarm didn't leave Caroline's room that night until she was sound asleep. He went discreetly across the hall to his room, being careful as he unlocked the door and went inside. More than once in his life, he had entered a hotel room only to have somebody shoot at him, and his experience at the bathhouse earlier in the evening was proof positive that somebody in Lodestone wanted him dead.

The room was empty, though, so he was able to undress and stretch out on the bed to get some sleep. He dozed off within minutes and spent the rest of the night in a deep, dreamless slumber.

The hectic activity of the day before insured that he was a mite stiff and sore when he woke up the next morning. A good breakfast and a couple of cups of coffee made him feel better. Caroline hadn't come down from her room yet, so when Longarm was finished with his meal, he went into the hotel lobby and told Stevens, "When Miss Thaxter comes down, tell her I've gone over to Marshal Flynn's office, would you?"

"Of course, Marshal." The hotel owner didn't seem so snippy this morning. The fact that the rest of the night had passed peacefully had probably helped him get over his irritation.

Longarm stepped out onto the hotel porch and paused to light a cheroot, snapping the lucifer to life with his thumbnail. Lodestone's main street was busier this morning, with several wagons rolling along it and pedestrians and horsebackers moving around as well. Longarm strolled across the street and down to the next block, where he found Artemus Flynn sitting on the porch of the marshal's office and jail. The local lawman had his chair tipped back and one foot propped against the railing at the edge of the porch.

Flynn greeted Longarm. "Morning, Marshal. I hope you didn't have any more trouble last night. I didn't get any reports of further ruckuses."

"Nope, no trouble," Longarm said as he leaned a hip against the porch railing.

"Glad to hear it. Maybe you won't have such a low opinion of our little town after all."

"Did you talk to Riley Bascomb and his pa yet?"

A frown creased Flynn's forehead. "As a matter of fact, I did," he said. "Hate to say it, but things went about like I expected. Riley claims he wasn't anywhere near Hukill's place yesterday evening, and Mayor Bascomb backs him up. He says Riley came home and stayed there after I talked to him." Flynn thumbed his hat back. "Matter of fact, Hugh—that's the mayor—isn't very happy that I didn't arrest you, Marshal."

"Because of that whipping I gave his boy?"

Flynn nodded. "That's right. Riley made it sound like you were to blame for everything. According to him, you jumped him when he wasn't doing anything."

"That's a damned lie," Longarm said with a snort of contempt for Riley Bascomb.

"You know that and I know that, and more importantly, you've got a witness to back up your story. Hugh calmed down a little when I told him about what Miss Thaxter said."

"Well, I appreciate you talking to them, Marshal, even if it didn't do any good."

"I expect you'll be leaving town today, after you've seen that outlaw's grave, so you shouldn't have any more trouble from Riley."

"Now that you mention it," Longarm said, "I may be staying around Lodestone for a day or two longer than I'd planned."

Flynn's eyebrows went up in surprise. "Really? You've got an idea where Hathaway cached that missing payroll?"

"Unfortunately, no. But I told Miss Thaxter that I'd give her a hand with the business that brought her here. Maybe you can help, too."

"And what business would that be?" Flynn asked. "The lady hasn't said anything to me about it. I've got to admit, I wondered a bit about why she was here."

"She's looking for her father."

"Is he supposed to live here? I don't recall anybody in town being named Thaxter—" Flynn stopped short and then said, "Oh, shit."

Longarm straightened from his casual pose. "What is it?" he asked. "You recognize the name after all, Marshal?"

"Yesterday, when I heard Miss Thaxter's name, I thought there was something familiar about it, but I couldn't quite remember what it was. Now you've jogged my memory. You happen to know what her father's first name was?"

Longarm caught that "was" and it made him even more uneasy. "Gordon," he said. "Gordon Thaxter." Caroline had told him her father's first name during their conversation in her room the night before, after she had "thanked" him for offering to help her.

Flynn sighed. "I was afraid that was what you were going to say."

"He was here, and something happened to him?" Longarm guessed.

"Remember that fella I told you about, the one who tried to break into one of the stores?"

"The one you had to shoot?" Longarm asked grimly.

"That's right. Marshal, I hate to say it, but Miss Thaxter's father is dead. He's buried up there in the graveyard, not far from that other outlaw, Nate Hathaway."

Chapter 10

Flynn wanted to go inside, rather than telling the story out on the porch, so he and Longarm moved into the office. When they were seated, Flynn behind the desk and Longarm straddling a ladderback chair in front of it, the local lawmen went on, "Like I mentioned last night, this fella tried to break in and rob one of the stores while I was making my rounds one night a couple of weeks ago. I was in front of the place when I heard glass break in the alley next to the building."

"He didn't know anybody was around?" Longarm asked.

"I reckon not, because he was pretty blatant about it. I drew my gun and stepped around the corner into the alley. Couldn't see very well because of the shadows back there, but I saw that busted window, all right. And then I saw an hombre about to climb in through it. I yelled at him to stop and put his hands up."

"He didn't elevate, though, did he?" Longarm guessed.

Regretfully, Flynn shook his head. "No, he turned toward me and grabbed his gun. Even then, I didn't shoot. I told him to drop it."

"That was taking a mighty big chance."

Flynn shrugged. "I don't like to fire my gun unless I

67

have to. When he let go with a round at me, I figured I didn't have any choice. I pulled the trigger and he went down."

"You weren't hit?"

"No, he rushed his shot," Flynn said. "It went wide. It's good to be fast, but I've always operated on the theory that it's better to be accurate."

Longarm knew that most lawmen felt the same way. He had been blessed with quickness of hand and eye, so he was both fast on the draw and deadly accurate with his shots, but not everybody was lucky enough to possess that skill.

"He didn't shoot again," Flynn went on, "so I ran up to him and lit a match. I saw that I'd drilled him in the heart, mostly by luck. He was already dead."

"What did you do then?"

"Went to fetch Edgar Horne and Lonnie. They carried him down to their place, and I went along to search his pockets. I found a couple of letters addressed to Gordon Thaxter, so that's how I know his name."

"Were those letters from his daughter?"

Flynn shook his head. "No. They were from a woman, but not his daughter. She was some gal in Kansas City, and from the, uh, personal nature of what she wrote, I figured she was his ladyfriend."

So Gordon Thaxter had had a woman on the side. Longarm decided that Caroline didn't need to know about that. She already had enough reasons to resent her late father. Of course, it was possible that Thaxter had taken up with the woman in Kansas City after his wife died, but according to Caroline, he hadn't known about that.

"I've still got the letters around here somewhere if you think Miss Thaxter would want them," Flynn continued.

Longarm shook his head. "I don't reckon that's necessary. You're sure the gent you shot was Thaxter? Maybe the letters didn't belong to him."

"Maybe not. I don't have any way of knowing about that. I can talk to Miss Thaxter, though, and give her the description of the man who was killed."

Longarm hated the thought of putting Caroline through that ordeal, but he didn't see any way around it. If her father was dead, she needed to know, so she could stop looking for him and go back home.

"I'll fetch her," he said. "She'll probably want to see the grave."

"Sure thing. I was going to take you up to the cemetery anyway, to show you where Hathaway is buried. We can all go up there together."

Longarm got to his feet. "I'll go over to the hotel and see if she's up yet. Be back in a spell."

"I'll be here," Flynn promised.

Once he was outside, Longarm dropped the butt of his cheroot in the street and ground it out with the toe of his boot. He walked to the hotel, went inside, and looked into the dining room when he saw that Caroline wasn't in the lobby. Sure enough, she was sitting at a table, having breakfast.

He was just about to ruin her morning, Longarm thought sadly.

Caroline looked up and greeted him with a smile. "Good morning, Custis," she said. "Mr. Stevens told me you'd gone to see Marshal Flynn, but I thought you'd probably be back soon. Have you had breakfast?"

"Yeah, I have," he said as he sat down in an empty chair and took off his hat.

"Well, then, how about just a cup of coffee? Did you sleep well last night?"

"Slept just fine," he said. "Mighty fine, in fact."

Caroline smiled, looked down at her plate, and blushed prettily. "I'd like to think that I had something to do with that."

"You did, no doubt about it." The waitress approached

the table with a cup and the coffeepot, but Longarm shook his head and waved her away.

That made Caroline frown a little. "Is something wrong, Custis?"

"I'm afraid so, and there ain't no getting around it."

She reached across the table and touched one of his hands. "Have you learned something about . . . my father?"

"I talked to Marshal Flynn and found out what you need to know. Your father was here a couple of weeks ago—"

"And he moved on already," Caroline guessed. She sighed. "I knew it. I had a feeling the trail wasn't going to end here. I swear, I don't know if I'm ever going to find him."

Longarm moved his hand so that Caroline's hand was clasped in his. "That's not it," he said. "Your father's still here." Quickly, so that the hope he saw dawning in her eyes wouldn't have time to take hold, he went on, "He was killed when he tried to rob one of the businesses. He took a shot at Marshal Flynn, and the marshal had to return fire."

Caroline blinked. Confusion had replaced hope in her eyes. "But . . . but that's not possible. He can't be dead."

"I'm afraid he is. He's buried up in the graveyard. Flynn said he'd show us the grave."

"But how does the marshal know the man was my father?" An edge of desperation had crept into Caroline's voice. She didn't want to give up the dream of finding her father alive.

"He found some papers on the man he shot, and they identified him as Gordon Thaxter. That was your pa's name, wasn't it?"

"Yes, but . . . surely it's a mistake! Just because a man had some papers with my father's name on them doesn't mean it was him!"

"The marshal and I talked about that," Longarm admitted. "He said if I'd bring you over to his office, he'd tell you what the man looked like."

Caroline sprang to her feet, the coffee that was still in her cup forgotten. "Yes, let's go right now, Custis." Her excitement was evident. She was still clinging to a shred of belief that her father could be alive.

Longarm hoped that would turn out to be the case. But his gut told him that it probably wouldn't be.

He tried to take her arm as they started across the street, but she pulled away. He couldn't blame her for being upset with him. After all, he had brought her some mighty bad news. Two years she had spent looking for her pa, only to discover that she had caught up with him two weeks too late. Now she was truly an orphan. That was a hard thing, even for a grown person.

Marshal Flynn stood up as they came through the door into the office. "Miss Thaxter," he said, "I'm really sorry. I guess Marshal Long has told you—"

Caroline broke in. "Marshal Long has told me that a man who was killed here a couple of weeks ago *might* have been my father. I don't believe it, though. I won't believe it until I hear for myself what he looked like."

Flynn looked miserable, and Longarm understood how he felt. Not only was the chore Flynn had to carry out now an unpleasant one, but he was also the person who had pulled the trigger and ended the life of this young woman's father. Flynn rubbed at his jaw and then said, "He was a tall man, on the slender side, with gray hair that looked like it might have been red when he was younger. He had green eyes."

That matched with Caroline's hair and eye coloring. There were a lot of green-eyed redheads in the world, though, so it didn't really prove anything, Longarm told himself.

"I don't remember seeing any scars," Flynn went on, "leastways not any that stood out. One thing I do recall, though, his ears . . . well, his ears were what you might call a little prominent."

Caroline lifted a hand to her mouth. Her eyes widened, and Longarm knew that part of the description meant something to her.

"Oh, no . . . ," she said in a half whisper. "My . . . my mother always said I had my father's eyes and hair, and she . . . she said thank God I didn't get his ears . . ."

Both hands covered her face, and she began to sob.

Longarm put his arms around her. She didn't resist this time as he drew her against him and put a hand on the back of her head. She balled her fists and dug them against his chest as her tears made his shirtfront wet.

The two men stood there in silence and let Caroline cry out her grief. After a while Longarm ventured a few pats on her back. Gradually her sobs diminished, and finally she was able to lift her head and say in a choked voice, "It's true. I know now it was him. It's really true."

"I can't tell you how sorry I am, Miss Thaxter," Flynn said. "Both to have to break the news to you, and because I reckon I'm the one who's to blame for what happened."

She shook her head. "No, Marshal. You may have pulled the trigger, but you weren't to blame. My . . . my father brought his fate on himself. I suppose it was inevitable . . . He was a criminal for many years . . . Things had to end badly for him."

"Maybe so, but I'm sorry I had to be the one who . . . Well, I'm sorry, that's all."

"So am I, Caroline," Longarm said.

"Can you . . . show me the grave, Marshal?"

"Sure," Flynn said. "You want to go up there now?"

"Yes, if you don't mind. I feel like I need to see it."

Flynn got his hat from the nail on the wall. "Come on, then. It won't take but a few minutes."

The three of them left the office, Caroline flanked by the two lawmen. Flynn led them to the church at the north end of the street. The building's whitewashed walls gleamed in the morning sunlight. A path ran beside the sanctuary and then a short distance up the hill to the cemetery.

The graveyard had a low wall around it built of mortar and red sandstone. At the entrance were two stone pillars with a wrought iron arch between them at the top. Formed in letters of iron were the words "LODESTONE CEMETERY." There were also wrought iron gates that could be closed off, but that were open at the moment.

As Longarm, Flynn, and Caroline walked in, the big federal lawman spotted a wagon parked farther into the graveyard. He saw a big man he recognized as Lonnie, undertaker Edgar Horne's helper, digging a grave.

Flynn saw Longarm looking at the big, hulking man and said, "Lonnie takes care of the cemetery, too, as well as giving Edgar a hand. When he stopped by the office this morning Doc Donaldson told me that old Mrs. Shelton passed away last night, so I reckon it's her resting place Lonnie's working on."

Longarm nodded. Lonnie gave them sort of a surly look as they went by, but that seemed to be his natural expression.

"Right here," Flynn said when they came to a fairly recent grave. A plain wooden marker stood at the head of it, with the name "Gordon Thaxter" burned into it, along with a date from two weeks earlier. "Nobody knew the, uh, date of birth," Flynn continued apologetically, "so I told Edgar just to put the date of, uh, death."

Caroline jerked her head in a nod. She clasped her hands together in front of her breast and stared down at the grave and the marker. Tears ran silently down her cheeks.

Longarm and Flynn took off their hats in a show of respect and stepped back to give her some privacy. Flynn said quietly, "If you'd like to see Hathaway's grave, Marshal, it's right over here."

"That'd be fine," Longarm said.

Flynn took him over to an even more freshly dug grave. Again, there was just a plain wooden marker with a name and date of death. In this case, the name was Calvin Johnson, even though Longarm knew it was really Nate Hathaway who was buried there.

"I reckon we could put up a new marker . . . ," Flynn said.

Longarm shook his head. "No need. I don't reckon anybody else will ever come here looking for Hathaway." He still had his hat in his hands. As he turned it over, he looked down at the grave and said, "Nate, I sure wish you could tell me where you hid that army payroll. I pure-dee hate to go back to Denver without it."

But there was no answer, of course. Whatever secrets Nate Hathaway had possessed, he had taken them on to the next world with him.

Chapter 11

Caroline came over to join Longarm and Flynn a few minutes later. She was wiping her eyes with a handkerchief and drying the tears on her face. She seemed to be in control of her emotions again.

"Thank you, Custis," she said. "And you, too, Marshal Flynn. You've both been very kind to me."

"It's generous of you to say so, ma'am," Flynn said. "This whole business still bothers me."

"You were just doing your job, and protecting your own life, as well," Caroline told him. "No one can hold that against you. I certainly don't."

Flynn just nodded his gratitude to her. There wasn't much left to say.

They walked back to the front gate of the cemetery, Longarm idly taking mental note of some of the names on the markers. They passed Lonnie again along the way. The sound of the shovel in the big man's hand biting into the soil grated on Longarm's nerves. He was glad when they were out of earshot of the grave-digging.

After they left Flynn at the marshal's office, Longarm and Caroline headed toward the hotel. She said, "I suppose there's no reason for either one of us to stay in Lodestone now. I'll start back to Trickham today. That's where the nearest railroad is, isn't it?"

Longarm nodded. "Yeah. San Angelo's closer, but the Texas Pacific ain't got there yet. The Santa Fe Railroad has a spur from Brownwood down to Trickham."

Caroline put a hand on his arm and said, "Would it be a terrible imposition if I were to ask you to ride there with me, Custis? I don't feel much like traveling alone anymore."

"I was already thinking about the same thing," he told her with a nod. "It'll take us a couple of days to get there, though. Won't do your reputation much good if folks hear about you spending a night on the trail with a man."

She summoned up a smile. "You think I'm worried about such things now? With my father gone, the only person whose opinion concerns me is you, Custis . . . and I certainly don't think you're going to object to spending some more time with me."

"You're right about that," he told her.

She was in mourning, though, so he would have to be careful of her feelings, he reminded himself. The important thing was that she didn't need to be alone right now.

She went on into the hotel to pack her things and get ready to leave, while Longarm walked down to the livery stable and told Ben Monklin that they would need the buggy horse hitched up. He took care of saddling his own horse.

"What about all them owlhoots' mounts that you brought in, Marshal?" the liveryman asked.

"You can work that out with Marshal Flynn," Longarm told him. "I don't have any call on them, or any use for them, either." He had already gone through all the saddlebags and hadn't found any of the army payroll or anything else of interest.

"Be sorry to see you go," Monklin said with a grin. "You been good for business, Marshal. Mine and Edgar Horne's, anyway."

"Reckon that's one thing there'll always be a need for," Longarm commented.

"A livery stable, you mean?"

"An undertaker," Longarm said.

It was mid-morning when Longarm stopped by the marshal's office to tell Flynn he and Caroline were leaving. He wanted to thank Flynn for his help and bid the local lawman farewell.

As soon as he walked in, he saw that Flynn already had a visitor. The man who sat in front of Flynn's desk was heavyset and dressed in a brown tweed suit. He had a round face under graying sandy hair. He was smiling when he turned toward Longarm, but the eyes set in pockets of fat were cold and unfriendly.

"Well, who's this?" the man asked in the hearty tone of a politician.

"Hugh, this is Marshal Custis Long," Flynn said with a worried frown, and Longarm wasn't a bit surprised at how Flynn addressed the man. He had already pegged the stranger's likely identity.

Mayor Hugh Bascomb didn't bother any longer with the pretense of a smile as he stood up and turned toward Longarm. He scowled as he said, "This is the man who attacked Riley?"

"That ain't quite the way it happened, Mayor," Longarm drawled, stepping in so that Flynn wouldn't have to answer. Flynn had treated him decently, and he didn't want the marshal caught in the middle of this mess.

"Listen here, Long," Bascomb went on. "I know from what Artemus tells me that you're a federal lawman, but that doesn't mean that you're above the law. You can't just come into a town and attack one of its leading citizens and expect to get away with it."

Flynn was on his feet now, too. "Hugh, take it easy," he said. "I told you, I investigated the matter, and I don't believe Marshal Long was guilty of any wrongdoing. Miss Thaxter told me—"

Bascomb cut him off with a sharp gesture from a pudgy hand. "Why you'd believe a trollop from out of town rather than my own son is beyond me, Artemus."

Longarm's jaw tightened. He moved a step closer to Bascomb and said, "I'd take it kindly, old son, if you'd apologize for that remark. You got no call to be insulting a lady."

"I won't apologize," Bascomb said with a defiant tilt of his chin. "And you can try to intimidate me all you want. I'm not afraid of you, Long."

Flynn came out from behind the desk in a hurry. "Damn it, both of you fellas settle down!" he ordered. "I'm not going to have a fistfight breaking out in the middle of my office!" With the aplomb of a man who had broken up plenty of potential fracases over the years, he moved smoothly between Longarm and Bascomb. He asked Longarm, "Did you want something, Marshal?"

"Yeah, to tell you so long. Miss Thaxter and I are leaving."

Bascomb snorted. "Good riddance to the both of you! You're nothing but troublemakers. We don't need your sort in Lodestone. This is—"

"A peaceable town, I know," Longarm said. He turned his attention back to Flynn and went on, "Thanks for your help, Marshal."

Flynn nodded. "You're welcome. Tell Miss Thaxter good-bye for me, will you?"

"Sure."

"Now, if that's all . . ."

Longarm had no trouble catching the hint. He said, "We'll be moving on." He gave Flynn a nod, then turned and walked out of the office.

"Don't think you've heard the last of this!" Bascomb shouted past Flynn. "I intend to file a complaint with your superior!"

Longarm ignored him. If Bascomb ever got around to

filing such a complaint, Henry would probably be appalled, but Billy Vail would know better than to put any stock in the rantings of a blustery small town politico.

The buggy was parked in front of the hotel. Caroline, wearing her traveling outfit again, stood on the porch, waiting. Longarm came up to her, smiled, and asked, "Ready to go?"

"Yes, I think so. I wouldn't mind stopping on the way out of town to say good-bye to Marshal Flynn—"

She broke off as Longarm began to shake his head. "I don't reckon that'd be a good idea," he told her. "I was just down at the marshal's office, and Mayor Bascomb is there with Flynn. He's pretty riled up over what happened to his boy."

"But it was his own fault," Caroline protested. "You were just defending me, and yourself."

"Bascomb don't see it that way. He got downright rude about it."

Caroline paled with anger. "Did he say anything about me?"

"Best you just get in the buggy," Longarm suggested. "Both of us will be better off if we forget about Lodestone."

After a moment, she shrugged in resignation. "You're probably right. I'll never forget this place, though. I can't."

Longarm knew what she meant. Lodestone was where her father had died, and he was buried here as well. Caroline would always have a connection to the place, whether she wanted it or not.

After helping her into the buggy, Longarm swung up onto the horse he had ridden from San Antonio. When they got to the railroad at Trickham, he would have to make arrangements to have the mount shipped back to Fort Sam Houston. Longarm would take the Santa Fe to Fort Worth and make rail connections there that would get him back to Denver.

So he and Caroline would have some time together not only on the trail, but also on the train ride between Trickham and Fort Worth.

"Marshal Flynn did say for me to tell you good-bye for him," Longarm said as Caroline picked up the reins.

"Part of me says that I should hate him, but I just can't bring myself to do that," she said. "It wasn't his fault."

"Nope, I don't reckon it was."

"Let's go. I've had enough of this town." She flicked the reins and got the horses moving. The buggy rolled down the street with Longarm riding alongside it.

He'd had enough of Lodestone, too, and if he never came back here, it would be just fine with him.

Chapter 12

Around the middle of the afternoon, they came to the creek where they had first met. Caroline pulled back on the reins and brought the buggy to a halt. She sat there with a wistful smile on her face as she looked at the pretty little stream lined with cottonwoods and pecan trees.

"I don't think I'll ever forget the look on your face when I drove up, Custis. Not that I was paying all that much attention to your face just then . . ."

"I was right surprised," said Longarm.

"But you were still a gentleman about the situation. I knew that immediately. I could tell you were a good man, in more ways than one."

She had to feel a little better now, or she wouldn't be flirting with him like this. Although she was naturally disappointed to learn that her father was dead, she hadn't seen him for the past two years, and even before that the relationship between them had been pretty sporadic. She would mourn for his passing, yes, but the depth of her grief wouldn't be the same as if they had always been close.

She certainly hadn't forgotten about his death, though. After they had forded the creek and started on east toward the railhead again, she said, "It's very difficult to think of my father dying in such a . . . a petty crime. I know it

81

sounds terrible to say this, but he robbed banks and held up trains from Texas to the Dakota Territory. It's not like he was Jesse James or anything like that, but . . . but being shot in a small town alley because he was trying to break into a general store . . . it doesn't seem right."

"Maybe he felt like he didn't have any choice," Longarm said. "We don't know what the circumstances were."

"No, of course not. It's just hard for me to believe, that's all."

No matter how much she resented the fact that her father had pretty much deserted her and her mother for long periods of time, she still felt some natural affection and even admiration for the man, Longarm mused. He might not have been a good parent, but he was Gordon Thaxter, the outlaw, and that was better than nothing.

They covered a good bit of distance during the afternoon but were still not quite halfway to Trickham when evening shadows began to gather. Longarm had kept an eye out for a ranch house where they could spend the night, but they hadn't come across any. That meant they would have to camp out, so he began looking for a suitable place.

He found one at the base of a wooded hill. A tiny creek ran beside the spot, which was level and grassy. They could spread their bedrolls here and sleep in relative comfort.

Longarm tended to the horses and built a fire, then Caroline cooked supper. He could have managed that, too—years of experience had turned him into a fair-to-middlin' trail cook—but she insisted. Over a simple but tasty supper of bacon and biscuits, Longarm said, "You must've spent one night out here by yourself on the way to Lodestone."

Caroline nodded. "Yes, I did."

"Weren't you scared?"

"Certainly. But I have a Winchester rifle in the back of the buggy, and if anyone or anything came along and gave me trouble, I'd have had a hot lead welcome for them."

He grinned at the bold, forthright statement. "You know, I believe you would," he said.

"Just because I've lived in a city most of my life, don't mistake me for some sort of shrinking violet, Custis. I can take care of myself. And when I want something, I don't mind going after it and getting it, whatever it takes." She paused, but only for a second. "Just like I want you to share my blankets tonight, and I'm not going to take no for an answer."

"Well, I don't know that I'm going to argue with you about that," Longarm said, "but you don't have to feel obligated—"

"I don't. Not in the least. And even though I'm sorry about . . . what we found in Lodestone . . . I still have my own life to live and I want to share part of it with you."

That sounded just fine to Longarm. They finished their supper, drank the last of the coffee, and cleaned up. As the fire died down to a red glow, Caroline stood next to the bedroll that Longarm had spread out and began taking off her clothes. There was nothing self-conscious or uncomfortable about it. Caroline looked like it was the most natural thing in the world to her.

Longarm watched her with undisguised admiration. In the fading firelight, her hair was like burnished copper and her skin had a healthy, ruddy glow. When she was nude, she stood there and smiled at him.

"Do you like what you see, Custis?"

"I like it a whole heap," Longarm said.

"Then come over here and show me how much."

Longarm went to her, shedding his own clothes as he did, and by the time he was naked, too, both of them were seized with an undeniable urgency. He drew her into his arms and kissed her hungrily.

She responded in kind, boldly sliding her tongue into his mouth as she reached down to caress his erect manhood. He cupped her left breast in his right hand, kneading the firm globe of female flesh and strumming the hard nipple with his thumb. She pulled harder and more frantically on his shaft, milking drops of moisture from it and spreading them around the crown with her palm.

"Now," she whispered as she leaned back. "Take me now, Custis."

He lowered her to the bedroll. She spread her legs wide, opening herself to him in sensuous invitation. Longarm moved between her thighs, holding himself there on hands and knees as she grasped his member and guided it to her opening. They merged with a thrust of hips from each of them. Her core was wet, and Longarm slid into her with no trouble, filling her with his massive organ.

His hips bobbed above hers as he pumped in and out of her. Her ankles drummed on the small of his back as spasms began to shake her almost right away. Longarm didn't let himself go, however. He held off his own climax and drove into her harder and harder, lifting her higher and higher toward the plateau. Tonight, since they were out here all alone, she didn't have to restrain herself. She cried out in passion and clutched at him, her hips bouncing frenziedly on the blanket. Climax after climax rocked her.

Finally, Longarm couldn't hold back any longer. His seed burst from him in white-hot jets, filling her chamber to overflowing. They were both drenched by the intermingling of heated juices.

When Longarm was drained at last, he lifted himself off of her, his now softening shaft sliding out of her. He sprawled on his belly on the blankets beside her and tried to catch his breath. Caroline was gasping, too. She rolled toward him, put a hand on the back of his neck, and rubbed the powerful muscles there.

"Custis, you don't know what meeting you has meant to me," she said.

"I reckon I can make a pretty good guess," he said, then let out a low groan of pleasure as she continued to massage his neck.

After a moment Caroline sat up and swung a leg over him, straddling his upper thighs as she worked her way down his back, kneading the muscles. Her fingers were skillful, and he groaned again as she reached his buttocks. He was so relaxed that he felt himself slipping into sleep.

That feeling of relaxation vanished, utterly and abruptly, when he heard a fallen branch crack somewhere on the hillside above them.

It was such a faint sound that while Longarm's keen hearing picked it up, Caroline missed it completely. She felt him go tense all over, though, and started to say, "Custis, what's—"

She cried out in surprise as he rolled over, throwing her to the side. He lunged toward his gunbelt, which was coiled on the saddle he had taken off his horse earlier. Even as his hand closed around the Colt's grips, he was already turning, bringing the gun around, lifting it to meet any threat that might come rushing out of the trees.

He was too late, though. Three dark shapes charged out of the shadows. A booted foot swung at Longarm's head in a vicious kick. He jerked aside in time to avoid the full force of the kick, which might have taken his head off his shoulders if it had landed solidly. The boot grazed along the side of his skull with enough force to send him sprawling on the ground. Rockets seemed to burst behind his eyes.

Instinct kept him moving, despite the fact that the kick to the head had almost knocked him out. He rolled over just as a gun blasted and a slug kicked up dirt from the ground, only inches away. Caroline screamed.

The sound of her terrified shriek galvanized Longarm. He surged to his feet as Colt flame bloomed once again in the darkness. A bullet snarled past his ear. Since he still held his gun, he triggered at the muzzle flash and was rewarded by a pained cry and the sight of one of the shadowy figures spinning off its feet.

A rush of footsteps behind him made him spin around.

One of the attackers lunged at him, swinging a club of some sort. Longarm ducked under the blow and tackled the man, driving him backward. Suddenly they were among the embers of the fire, and the coals blistered Longarm's bare feet. He yelled in pain and heaved, upending his opponent so that the man fell in the scattered fire. Longarm rolled to the side, away from the searing pain.

The man he had dumped in the fire screeched and rolled the other way. In a furious rage, the man came up blazing away wildly with the gun in his hand.

Longarm couldn't return the shots, because he had dropped his Colt during the struggle. And now, with the campfire scattered and just about out, darkness closed in around him. He couldn't see Caroline anymore, or the men who had jumped them, either.

He crouched, trying to stay out of the line of fire. The hombre with the gun finally stopped shooting when the hammer clicked on an empty chamber in the cylinder. Longarm felt around until he found one of the rocks he and Caroline had used to surround the fire. Drawing back his arm, he let fly with the stone at the spot where the gunner had been a second earlier.

The man hadn't moved. Longarm knew that a second later when he heard the rock strike flesh and heard the man grunt in pain. There was no way of knowing, though, how much damage he had actually done.

Suddenly, with a pounding of hoofbeats, several horses burst out of the trees. One of the men must have gone back for their mounts. "Over here!" a voice yelled, and Longarm thought it sounded familiar. He ran in that direction.

A huge dark shape loomed over him like some sort of prehistoric monstrosity. He realized an instant later that it was a man on horseback, struggling with something or someone. A low cry told him that the man had hold of Caroline and was trying to keep her in front of him on the horse.

Longarm leaped toward them, but even as he did so, another rider slammed into him from the side, more than likely by accident in the dark. "It's him!" a man shouted, and a gun roared practically in Longarm's face. At the same time the horse hit him again and knocked him off his feet. He went over backward, his head slamming hard into something when he hit the ground.

Stunned by the impact, Longarm couldn't do anything except lie there and struggle to hang on to his rapidly fading senses. He heard the rataplan of swift hoofbeats fading into the distance. The three men were getting away, and they likely had Caroline with them as their prisoner.

That thought forced Longarm to move. He tried to get up, but his head spun dizzily and his strength deserted him. His muscles went limp, dumping him back on the ground. A futile curse grated from his mouth.

Then a darkness deeper than the night closed in around him and everything faded away, including the sounds of flight from the men who had stolen Caroline Thaxter away from him.

Chapter 13

When he regained consciousness, the pain told Longarm he was still alive. He lay there for seemingly endless moments, waiting for the agony in his head to recede. Something, some half-forgotten bit of memory, nagged at him, telling him it was urgent that he wake up and get moving.

But it was easier to just lie there, drowning in a sea of blackness shot through with streaks of red every time his pulse beat and pain throbbed inside his skull.

Then he remembered Caroline, and his eyes came open and a groan escaped between his tightly clenched teeth.

Fingers, toes, arms, legs . . . his muscles worked, reluctantly at first but then with greater ease. He opened his eyes and saw nothing above him except the stars. After a moment he was able to roll onto his side and then sit up.

Gingerly, he lifted a hand to the back of his head and felt the sticky lump there. He had walloped himself a good one when he fell, probably landing on a rock. It was just good luck he hadn't busted his head wide open. He didn't know how long he had been unconscious, but instinct told him he hadn't been out for long.

Long enough, though, for the horses carrying his enemies to be completely out of earshot. The night was quiet again except for the usual small sounds.

Grunting with the effort, Longarm climbed to his feet and shuffled around until he found his shirt. Digging in the pockets, he found some matches and snapped one of the lucifers to life with an iron-hard thumbnail. It flared up, nearly blinding him for a second. Then his eyes narrowed and adjusted, and he oriented himself. He saw the rest of his clothes scattered on the ground, along with the gun he had dropped. He shook out the match and got to work getting dressed.

He couldn't go after those bastards buck naked.

There was no question that he was going after them, of course. They had done their damnedest to kill him, and they had kidnapped Caroline. Either of those things was bad enough. Taken together they guaranteed that Longarm was going to track them down and make them pay for what they'd done.

He was moving very slowly, and the delay chafed at him. He fought down the feeling of impatience. As shaky as he still was, if he tried to hurry he might fall flat on his face, and that would just make it even longer before he could start after Caroline and her captors.

Finally he had his clothes on and his gunbelt buckled around his hips. He picked up his hat and tried to put it on, but the lump on his head was too tender and painful for that. Disgustedly, he tossed the flat-crowned, snuff-brown Stetson into Caroline's buggy, which was still parked next to the camp. The attackers hadn't tried to take the vehicle. It would have just slowed them down, and they had been in a hurry.

That must have been why they hadn't taken the time to make sure Longarm was dead, too. They were going to regret that oversight, he vowed.

The buggy horses and Longarm's saddle mount were still tied to a sturdy little post oak tree. He was glad his horse hadn't bolted because of its skittishness around gunfire. If the shooting had continued for much longer, it probably would have.

Still moving deliberately, but a little faster now, Longarm got the horse ready to ride. His Winchester was snugged in the saddle boot. He put his left foot in the stirrup and swung up on the animal's back.

Now he just had to figure out which way to go.

He frowned in concentration. He was pretty sure the riders had been headed north when they galloped away from the camp. That would take them toward the Brady Mountains and the Colorado River. Pretty rugged country up there, with lots of wooded hills and brush-choked ravines. They would have plenty of places to hide while they did whatever they planned to do to Caroline. Longarm wouldn't let himself think too much about that.

The men couldn't move very fast. They had Caroline to contend with, and Longarm figured she wouldn't cooperate. In fact, she would probably be a struggling, spitting, redheaded fury.

And one of the bastards was wounded, too. Longarm had seen the man fall to his shot, and when he'd lit that match, he had seen a splash of blood on the ground. He had no way of knowing how badly the man was hurt, but he probably hadn't been able to maintain a gallop for very long.

So Longarm was left with at least the hope of catching up to them. If they turned and headed another direction, though, he wouldn't be able to tell it in the dark. He ran the risk of losing their trail altogether.

The alternative was to wait until morning and track them in a more traditional manner. But that option was fraught with risk, too. It would mean giving them hours and hours in which to build a lead on him. Depending on what they planned to do to Caroline, he might not catch up to them in time to help her. She might already be dead.

But they wouldn't kill her for a while, he told himself. Bastards like that would want to have some fun with her first, which meant they would have to stop somewhere. If his guess was correct, he stood a better chance of catching them if he just rode north and kept his eyes and ears open.

Years of listening to his hunches had taught Longarm that they were right more often than not. He clucked to his horse and heeled the animal into a trot, heading north and steering by the stars.

For a while, every time the horse's hooves struck the ground it sent a sharp jolt of pain through Longarm's head. The agony gradually dulled to a miserable ache, and he was able to ignore it. He moved at a steady pace. The moon and stars cast enough light so that from time to time he saw a hoofprint on the ground. That gave him hope.

He had covered several miles when he spotted a tiny glow ahead of him. It might be the light from a window of some isolated ranch house or farmer's homestead. There might even be a little settlement up there.

Or it might be a campfire. Caroline's captors might have stopped, thinking themselves safe from pursuit. Longarm recalled the gunshot that had gone off practically in his face, so close that he had felt the sting of burning powder on his cheek. He had gone down as soon as the deafening blast roared out, knocked off his feet by one of the horses. It could be that the attackers believed the shot had blown his brains out, even though the bullet had missed him completely.

That sort of arrogant overconfidence fit perfectly with the man he suspected of being behind the attack. Again, Longarm's gut told him that his hunch was right.

But there was only one way to find out for sure, so he kept his gaze fixed on that distant spot of light and rode toward it steadily.

By the time he was only a few hundred yards away, he could tell that the light came from a small fire. He reined in and swung down from the saddle. He needed to go the rest of the way on foot, so they wouldn't hear the horse and know he was coming. After he had tied the reins to a mesquite bush, he slid the rifle out of the saddle boot and worked the lever, jacking a round into the Winchester's firing chamber.

Then, with a stealth and grace uncommon in such a big man, he catfooted toward the fire.

His head didn't hurt anymore, or if it did, he didn't think about it. All his attention was focused on approaching the camp quietly. As he drew nearer, he smelled the woodsmoke, and closer still, he suddenly heard the harsh sound of a man's laughter.

Something about the laugh made Longarm's jaw tighten and the hair on the back of his neck stand up. He dropped into a crouch and moved forward as silently as an Indian.

The camp was in a clearing with trees on one side and brush on the other. A log and a couple of small boulders formed seats for the four people gathered around the fire. One of them was Caroline. She clutched a blanket around her shoulders, but judging by the large expanses of bare flesh that appeared under it whenever she moved, the blanket was her only garment.

Her head was down, so that she stared at the ground. She paid no attention to the coarse comments of the three men, most of which concerned how pretty she was and how much fun they were going to have with her. Longarm had to rein in the fierce anger he felt as Caroline's captors spewed their vileness. He would have a better chance of rescuing her and bringing these bastards to justice if he remained calm.

One of them was Riley Bascomb. That came as no surprise to Longarm. He had thought that he recognized Riley's voice back there at the other camp, during the fight, and Riley was just the sort of sneaky son of a bitch who would try to take his revenge by attacking his enemies from out of the dark.

Riley wouldn't draw a line at molesting a woman, either, and obviously neither would his two companions. They weren't dressed as well as he was and looked rougher, but there was no doubt that Riley was the boss. The other two were probably cowboys from some ranch near Lodestone who were Riley's drinking buddies. He might have promised to pay them for helping him avenge himself on Longarm and Caroline, or they might have come along just for the cruel fun of it.

Either way, one of the men had gotten more than he bargained for, because he had a bloody bandage tied around the upper part of his right arm. That had to be where Longarm's bullet had ventilated him. Wounded or not, though, he looked at Caroline with the same sort of lustful avarice as the other two.

Riley sat beside Caroline on the log. The other two men perched on rocks. Riley reached over and tugged on the blanket that Caroline clutched around herself. "Come on, darlin'," he said with a smirk. "It's a warm night. You don't need to wrap up."

She pulled away from him. "When Marshal Long catches up to you—" she began.

Riley interrupted her with a laugh. "That damn marshal ain't gonna catch up to nobody. Cole's gun was right in his face when he pulled the trigger. Long went down like a poleaxed steer. His brains are splattered all over that campsite."

A grim smile touched Longarm's mouth for a second. His hunch had been right. They were sure he was dead.

They were about to pay for that mistake.

Riley pulled harder at the blanket, baring one of Caroline's breasts. She caught her breath and sat tensely on the log but didn't attempt to cover herself again. Longarm figured she was trying to resign herself to what she thought was inevitable.

The horses were tied to his right, about twenty feet away from the fire. He bent down, felt around on the ground until he found a small rock, and then straightened to toss it at the horses. The rock hit the rump of one of the animals, making it shy away suddenly. That caused it to bump against another horse, and suddenly all three of the mounts were skittish.

Riley's head came up sharply as he heard the commotion. "Damn it, why're those horses acting up?" he muttered.

"Might be a coyote skulkin' around out there," suggested the wounded man.

"Yeah," Riley agreed. "Go take a look, Cole."

The third man frowned. "Why me?"

"Bradford's hurt," Riley said, gesturing toward the wounded man, "and I got to keep this little honey here company." He put a hand on Caroline's bare shoulder and caressed it, coming close to the swell of her breast.

From his concealment, Longarm saw the little shudder that went through her. One more mark against Riley Bascomb, he told himself.

The man called Cole stood up. Grumbling, he walked away from the fire to check on the horses. Longarm circled quietly, moving to intercept him. As Cole paused beside the horses, speaking to them in an attempt to calm them, Longarm stepped up behind him and drove the butt of the Winchester against the back of his neck.

Cole folded up without a sound. Longarm caught him around the waist and lowered him to the ground so that Riley and Bradford wouldn't hear him fall.

Riley was already getting antsy, though. He called, "Cole? You see anything out there?"

Longarm knew there was no point in waiting. He had cut the odds against him by one, and with that wounded arm Bradford wouldn't be able to use a gun very well, if at all. With the Winchester leveled, Longarm stepped into the circle of light from the campfire, drew a bead on Riley, and said, "Go ahead and try something, Bascomb. I'd love an excuse to blow your head plumb off."

Chapter 14

"Custis!" Caroline cried out in surprise and relief.

As much as Longarm wanted to, he didn't look at her. Instead he kept his attention centered on Riley Bascomb as he said, "Caroline, get up and come over here. Don't get between me and Bascomb, though."

She came to her feet, still holding the blanket tightly about her, and began working her way around the campfire away from Riley.

"Long!" Riley said, and he put as much hatred into the word as Longarm had ever heard before. "I thought you were dead!"

"You can see for yourself that I ain't," Longarm said. "Not for any lack of trying by you and your pards, though."

"Where's Cole?" Riley demanded.

"Don't worry about him. He's back there in the brush, out cold, but he'll be all right to stand trial for kidnapping and attempted murder, just like the two of you."

Bradford, the wounded man, licked his lips nervously. Suddenly, he lunged at Caroline, who had come within reach of him as she tried to reach Longarm's side. Longarm had considered Bradford the lesser danger, but obviously the man still had some fight in him. He grabbed Caroline around the waist with his good arm and jerked her in front of him as she uttered a short scream of surprise and fear.

"Don't shoot, Marshal!" Bradford said as the barrel of Longarm's Winchester swung toward him. "You fire and you'll hit the girl!"

"Let her go, old son," Longarm grated. He could see part of Bradford's face as the man peered out from behind Caroline, but not enough to risk a shot.

"The hell with that! I ain't goin' to prison! You let me go or I'll kill her!"

"You hurt her and I'll kill you, right here and now," Longarm warned.

The thing that Longarm most worried about happened just then, as Riley Bascomb threw himself off the log in a dive that took him in the opposite direction from Bradford. Longarm was caught between them now. He snapped the rifle back toward Riley, because Bradford didn't have a gun out yet and Riley had drawn his as he rolled across the ground. The revolver in Riley's fist spat flame.

Longarm triggered the Winchester as he felt the tug of Riley's bullet on his shirt. Riley cried out, but Longarm didn't know if he had actually hit the young man or just come close. He darted back a couple of steps as he levered the rifle, trying to put himself at a better angle as he turned toward Bradford.

He was surprised to see Caroline hurtling straight toward him. Bradford had given her a hard shove that sent her careening forward out of control. The blanket fluttered around her, revealing most of her naked flesh. Meanwhile Bradford struggled to reach across his body and draw his gun with his left hand.

Caroline crashed into Longarm. His arms were suddenly full of nude, terrified woman. The impact knocked him back a step, and one of his feet came down on a small stone that rolled underneath him. He felt his balance desert him and he went over backward, taking Caroline with him.

The fall may have saved their lives, because Riley's gun blasted twice more and sent slugs screaming through the space where Longarm and Caroline had been an instant earlier.

Longarm landed on his back with Caroline on top of him. His left arm was around her, and the Winchester was still clutched in his right hand. He tipped the barrel up and fired it one-handed at the only target he had right then—the wounded man called Bradford.

The rifle bullet drove into the hardcase's chest just as Bradford finally got his own revolver drawn. He didn't have a chance to fire it. The bullet from Longarm's Winchester smashed him backward.

Longarm saw Bradford go down and knew the man was either dead or hit so hard that he was out of the fight. But that still left Riley, who was probably the most dangerous of all. Longarm rolled over so that Caroline was on the ground, and he hissed, "Stay down!" at her.

He started to come up in a crouch and Riley's gun roared again. The bullet whined past Longarm's head. The muzzle flash in the brush gave away Riley's position. As Longarm rolled across the ground, he fired three times, working the Winchester's lever between rounds. The spray of lead wasn't really intended to hit Riley, just to make him keep his head down until Longarm reached the cover of the log that Riley and Caroline had been using for a seat a few minutes earlier.

When he got there, Longarm saw to his relief that Caroline had had the sense to crawl behind one of the small boulders. She huddled there now, reasonably safe from Riley's bullets.

Longarm's pulse hammered in his head as he tried to figure out what Riley would do next. The young man could continue the gunfight and take his chances, or he could make a try for the horses and attempt to get away. Longarm decided the latter course of action was the most likely. Riley's cronies were out of the fight, and he wasn't the sort who liked it when the odds weren't heavily in his favor. He would prefer to run now and try to settle the score again later.

That line of thinking was why Longarm was already swinging the barrel of his rifle toward the horses when he saw Riley erupt from the brush and lunge toward the tethered animals. The light from the fire was dim, but it was good enough. Riley fired the gun in his hand wildly as he ran, trying to distract Longarm, but the big lawman ignored the hail of lead. He drew a bead and fired.

Riley cried out, spun halfway around, and toppled off his feet, carried forward a little by his momentum. Longarm saw the gun sail out of his hand.

Longarm was up and running toward the fallen man a second later, keeping the rifle trained on Riley as he approached. Riley writhed around on the ground and clutched at his right thigh.

"You shot me!" he shouted in apparent astonishment. "Damn you, Long, you shot me!"

Longarm stood over him and took some vague satisfaction in the sight of the blood on Riley's leg. "You're lucky I just winged you," he said grimly. "I could've put that slug right through your vitals."

Then he leaned over and smashed the rifle butt against Riley's head. With a strangled groan, Riley stretched out on the ground, unconscious.

That wound in Riley's leg would have to be tied up so that he wouldn't bleed to death, and Longarm wasn't going to take a chance on doing it while the bastard was awake. Riley was too tricky for that.

He turned his head and called, "Caroline, you all right?"

"I'm fine, Custis," she replied. "Can I come out now?"

"Yeah, get over here," he told her. When she came up with the blanket wrapped around her again, he handed her the Winchester. "You said you had a rifle like this in your buggy. I reckon you know how to use one?"

She let the blanket drape loosely around her shoulders as she took the Winchester. "I certainly do."

Longarm pointed toward the horses. "The other fella is lying over there. I knocked him out, but he might come to, so you'd better keep an eye on him. If he wakes up, show him that rifle. If he tries to move, shoot the son of a bitch. Can you do that?"

"He had better not try me and find out," Caroline said, and Longarm believed her.

With that taken care of, Longarm knelt beside Riley and began tending to his wound. He pulled the bandanna from the young man's neck, found a broken branch, and used the two items to make a tourniquet around Riley's leg and slow the bleeding. Then he pulled a clasp knife from his pocket and cut away the bloodstained trouser leg to expose the wound.

The bullet had gone in and out, resulting in an injury that wasn't much worse than a deep graze. Messy and painful enough to knock a man out of action, but not life-threatening providing that blood poisoning didn't set in. Longarm looked in the saddlebags on the men's horses and not surprisingly found a flask of whiskey in one of them.

He poured the whiskey over Riley's leg, drenching the wound in the fiery liquor. Even in his unconscious state, the pain of that made Riley shift around and moan. Better that than having his leg rot off, though. Once Longarm had cleaned the wound, he tore several strips of cloth off of Riley's shirt and used them to bind up the injury. He drew the makeshift bandages tight before he loosened the tourniquet. The bandages darkened a little, but the bleeding seemed to have stopped for the most part.

With that done, Longarm rolled Riley onto his belly, took the young man's belt, and used it to lash his hands together behind his back. When Riley came to, he wouldn't be able to cause any trouble.

"Any problems over there?" he called to Caroline.

"This one's starting to wake up," she said.

Longarm strode over to her and saw that Cole was indeed stirring on the ground. Before the man could fully regain his senses, Longarm rolled him over and tied his hands with his belt, too.

"Wha . . . what's goin' on?" Cole asked groggily as he twisted his neck and tried to look up at his captors.

"Just take it easy, old son," Longarm told him. "You're all right except for a headache. You want to keep it that way, you won't cause no trouble."

"M-Marshal Long?"

"That's right."

Cole ripped out a curse. "That bastard Riley's really got us up Shit Creek without a paddle, don't he?"

"Like I said, you're still alive. Behave yourself and you'll probably stay that way."

Cole sighed. "Whatever you say, Marshal." He added, "I sure as hell thought you were dead."

"That was your second mistake," Longarm told him.

"What was the first?"

"Listening to Riley Bascomb."

Chapter 15

Bradford was dead, just as Longarm suspected. Longarm rolled the corpse in a blanket. He thought about making Cole dig a grave so that they could bury Bradford right here, but in the end he decided to take the body on into Trickham, along with Caroline and the two prisoners.

"Are we going to stay here tonight?" Caroline asked. She was wearing Longarm's spare shirt now, along with a pair of denim trousers he had found in one of the saddlebags. The shirtsleeres and the pant legs were all rolled up considerably.

"We might as well," Longarm said in reply to her question. "It's a decent camp, and there's no point in traipsing across country in the dark. Come morning, we'll ride back down to the spot where you and I were camped and pick up your buggy. Even getting a late start like that, we ought to make it to Trickham by nightfall."

Riley and Cole lay near the fire where Longarm had dragged them. After coming to, Riley had cussed Longarm in a low, monotonous voice for several minutes before Longarm threatened to wallop him again. That shut him up.

Longarm drew Caroline off to the side and asked her in a low voice, "They didn't hurt you, did they?"

She shook her head. "They hadn't gotten around to it

yet. It wouldn't have been much longer, though, if you hadn't shown up when you did, Custis." She put her arms around him and rested her head against his chest. "They told me you were dead," she went on in a voice choked with emotion. "They said you'd been shot in the head. I . . . I didn't know what to do. I could hardly believe it. Something told me you'd be coming for me."

"It was a near thing," Longarm said. "We're both lucky they didn't put a few bullets in me for good measure. Reckon they were just too worked up to take the time to do that."

He held Caroline for a few minutes, both of them enjoying the closeness and drawing strength from each other.

Then Longarm said, "It's mighty late. You'd better get some sleep."

"After everything that's happened, I don't know if I'll be able to sleep," Caroline said with a little smile.

When she rolled up in some blankets, though, she dozed off almost right away, Longarm noted. He was glad that she was able to rest.

He sat up most of the night, smoking cheroots and keeping an eye on Riley and Cole. The prisoners slept, too, but once Riley woke up and looked across the dying fire at Longarm with sheer hatred burning in his eyes.

"You're going to be sorry you ever crossed my trail, Long," he said.

Longarm grunted. "Reckon I already am."

"No, I mean it. When my father finds out what you've done, he'll make you pay. You don't know who you're dealing with, you stupid bastard."

"Shut up," Longarm said. "My head hurts too much to listen to your bullshit."

"Just you remember what I said. You'll be sorry."

Riley glared at Longarm until he went back to sleep, leaving the big lawman alone with the small night sounds and his own thoughts. Something was bothering Longarm, an annoying tickle in the back of his brain that had nothing to do with the clout on the head he had suffered earlier in the night. This wasn't physical but mental, a nagging sensation that something was wrong.

He had heard or seen something that wasn't right. But try as he might, he couldn't figure out what it was.

All he knew for sure was that for some reason, his thoughts kept turning back to Lodestone, as if he had unfinished business there.

In the morning, Caroline fixed up a little breakfast from supplies that Longarm had in his saddlebags. Riley and Cole wanted to be turned loose to eat, but Longarm decided against it. Caroline fed them instead, refusing Longarm's offer to take care of that chore himself.

"I don't mind," she said. "I'd rather be feeding them poison than flapjacks, but I suppose one can't have everything."

That comment seemed to have an effect on the prisoners' appetites. They didn't eat much.

After breakfast Longarm saddled all the horses. He slung Bradford's blanket-wrapped corpse over one of the animals and tied it in place. Then he lifted Riley and Cole into their saddles. Riley complained that Longarm's rough treatment hurt his wounded leg.

"I already halfway wish I'd let you bleed to death, old son," Longarm warned him. "You better not push it."

Riley fell into a surly silence.

Longarm swung up into his own saddle and gave Caroline a hand as she climbed in front of him. His horse could carry double back to the other camp. Longarm didn't intend to travel at a very fast pace. It wasn't necessary.

They rode south. Longarm had tied lead ropes to the other horses so that Riley or Cole couldn't try to take off for the tall and uncut. They got an early start, so it wasn't yet mid-morning when they reached the spot where Longarm and Caroline had planned to camp the night before. The buggy and the two horses that went with it were still there. Apparently no one had bothered them during the night.

The lump on Longarm's head had gone down enough this morning so that he was able to put on his hat, which he retrieved from the buggy. He hitched up the buggy team while Caroline retreated into the bushes to change back into her own clothes. Riley made a couple of lewd comments while she was gone, until Longarm turned the barrel of the Winchester toward him. More and more, Longarm was regretting his decision to just wing Riley the night before, instead of killing him.

When Caroline emerged from the bushes in her dark green traveling outfit, she smiled at Longarm and said, "This is much better. No offense, Custis. I enjoyed wearing your shirt."

"And you made it look better than I ever did," he told her with a smile. "Ready to go?"

"Yes, I certainly am."

They pushed on eastward toward the railhead. It was a pretty day, warm with a decent breeze to keep the heat from building up too much. White clouds floated in the sky overhead. There hadn't been any rain in the area since the downpour a few days earlier.

At midday they stopped for a better lunch than the breakfast they'd had. By late afternoon, Longarm had spotted several ranch houses and quite a few cattle, and the trail they had been following turned into a regular road. A short time later, they crossed the Colorado River on a high plank bridge, and then rolled into the settlement of Trickham.

At one time the place had had a reputation as a hell-roaring cow town. Cattle baron John Chisum, now one of the most powerful ranchers in New Mexico Territory and a man who had crossed paths with Longarm several times, had gotten his start here in Texas a couple of decades earlier. Chisum had established his Jinglebob ranch near Trickham before moving his spread lock, stock, and barrel to New Mexico several years later. Other cattlemen had followed Chisum's example but remained in the Trickham area instead of leaving.

The arrival of the Santa Fe Railroad in the form of a spur line from Brownwood had civilized Trickham to a certain extent. So had the presence of a deputy who worked for the Coleman County sheriff. Trickham was still known as the home of some of the toughest hombres in this part of Texas, but mostly they did their hell-raising in other places these days.

Longarm reined his horse to a stop in front of the deputy's office and motioned for Caroline to bring the buggy to a halt. Bradford's body, not to mention the two prisoners, attracted quite a bit of attention from people on the street. Just as in Lodestone, there was nothing like riding in with a corpse to make folks perk up and take notice.

The deputy came out of the office while Longarm was hauling Riley and Cole down from their mounts. He was a tall, rawboned man with a ready grin and dark hair under his thumbed-back Stetson. He looked at the prisoners and the unmistakable shape wrapped in the blanket and said to Longarm in a friendly voice, "Had some trouble, did you, friend?"

"That's right," Longarm said. He looked at the star pinned on the man's vest and went on, "You'd be the deputy sheriff?"

"Yep. Name's Norm Duncan. Who might you be?"

"Deputy U. S. Marshal Custis Long."

Duncan let out a low whistle. "Federal star packer, eh?"

"That's right." Longarm jerked a thumb at Riley and Cole. "These boys here have broken some state laws, though, namely kidnapping and attempted murder."

"That's a damned lie!" Riley burst out. "He's the one who's a criminal. He's a madman who keeps trying to kill me!"

Duncan looked at Longarm with narrowed eyes, but his voice was still friendly, at least on the surface, as he asked, "You got any identification, Marshal?"

"Yeah, and a witness," Longarm replied with a nod toward Caroline. "Why don't we lock these hombres up, and then I'll show you my bona fides and Miss Thaxter and I can tell you what happened."

Duncan nodded. "Sounds fine to me."

Angrily, Riley began, "Listen, you two-bit tin-star—"

Duncan stopped him with an upraised hand. "If you want to convince me you're tellin' the truth, son, you're sure goin' about it the wrong way. Just settle down and don't give me any trouble. If you've got a story to tell, I'll hear it later."

With that, Duncan and Longarm marched the prisoners inside. Caroline followed them. Longarm said, "The one who's wounded ought to have a sawbones take a look at his leg. I reckon you've got an undertaker here for the hombre we left outside?"

"I'm sure somebody's already gone to fetch him," Duncan replied with a nod.

There were two small cells behind the deputy's office. The lawmen put the prisoners there, one in each cell, after untying their hands. Back in the office, Duncan said to Longarm, "All right, Marshal, let's hear it."

Longarm handed over the leather folder containing his badge and identification papers, and then he quickly laid out the events of the past few days for the deputy sheriff, leaving out only the intimate details that would embarrass Caroline unnecessarily. She corroborated his story, her voice ringing with conviction as she told how Riley, Cole, and Bradford had attacked them, nearly killed Longarm, and carried her off as a captive.

"I'd tell you the vile things they said and how they threatened me," she concluded, "but I can't bring myself to repeat them."

"That's all right, ma'am, you don't have to," Duncan assured her. "Where did all this villainy take place?"

"About halfway between here and Lodestone," said Longarm.

Duncan frowned. "That's over in Concho County, across the county line. Maybe even in Tom Green County, since I ain't exactly sure of the location. I don't know if I have the jurisdiction to hold those fellas, Marshal."

"You can hold them at the request of a federal lawman until I've had a chance to wire the sheriffs of Concho and Tom Green Counties and figure out what to do with them," Longarm said.

Duncan rubbed his jaw in thought and then slowly nodded. "Yeah, I reckon I could do that. My boss would want me to cooperate with you."

"I'm obliged. You've got a telegraph office here in town?"

"Sure do," Duncan said with a touch of pride in his voice. "Telegraph line came in when the railroad did."

"Speaking of the railroad," Caroline put in, "when is the next train due?"

"A couple of days from now," replied Duncan. "It only runs twice a week."

"I knew that. I came through here about a week ago."

"Yes, ma'am, I thought you looked a mite familiar. Part of my job is to keep up with who gets on and off the train."

Duncan grinned. "I tend to remember owlhoots and pretty girls best of all." He sat up straighter in the chair behind the desk and grew more serious. "Speakin' of which . . . Marshal, you didn't happen to see this fella while you were over there at Lodestone, did you?"

He picked up a reward dodger and handed it to Longarm.

With a frown on his face, Longarm studied the drawing of a man's face and the printing on the poster. "Silver Jack Meehan," he said. "Wanted for bank robbery and murder. Seems like I've heard the name, but I don't recollect ever seeing him. Not in Lodestone, anyway."

Duncan shrugged as he took back the reward dodger. "Reason I ask is that I spotted him gettin' off the train here a few days ago. I thought I recognized him, but I wasn't sure so I came back here to the office to check the poster. When I saw I was right, I went to round him up, but he was already gone. He stopped just long enough to get a drink in one of the saloons and then bought a horse and rode out."

"Did you try to pick up his trail and go after him?"

"Thought about it," Duncan said, "but he was spotted heading toward the river, and that's the county line. There's that pesky jurisdiction problem again."

"What makes you think he might have been bound for Lodestone, other than the direction he rode off?"

"Because he asked in the saloon how to find the place," Duncan said. "Told the bartender he had business there." The deputy sheriff shrugged again. "But I reckon it ain't any of your worry, Marshal, seein' as how you're a federal lawman and all. Far as I know, Silver Jack ain't wanted by the federal government."

That might be true, but as Longarm looked down at the other reward posters scattered on Duncan's desk, he stiffened, and what felt like an icy finger trailed along his spine.

He knew, right then and there that, whether he wanted to or not, he would be going back to Lodestone . . .

Chapter 16

Longarm kept his suspicions to himself as he took Caroline over to the hotel and got rooms for both of them. He wasn't sure what to tell her about the idea that had occurred to him while they were in the deputy sheriff's office. She might take it as good news—or she might not.

He would have to tell her *something*, though, because his plans had changed and he would no longer be accompanying her on the train when it pulled out for Brownwood, Fort Worth, and points north and east.

They met in the hotel dining room for supper. Caroline had changed into a light blue gown that looked particularly fetching on her. She didn't seem any the worse for the previous night's ordeal, and he admired her resilience as well as her beauty.

"You look mighty nice tonight," he told her.

She blushed prettily. "Thank you, Custis. So do you."

"Shoot, I didn't do anything except wash up, shave, and put on a clean shirt. I'm still just a rough ol' cowboy."

Caroline reached across the table and rested her hand on his. "As you might say, Custis, not hardly."

He grinned at her. He was going to miss her, once he started back to Lodestone.

The trip couldn't be avoided, though. He knew he would never rest until he had put his mind at ease.

After they ate, they walked back across the white-tiled floor of the lobby to the stairs. Caroline slipped her hand into his as they went up to the second floor. Longarm knew perfectly well what was about to happen and didn't bother to resist it. No sane man would have.

They wound up in her room, where they slowly and methodically divested each other of clothes. Longarm enjoyed undressing a beautiful woman, and Caroline Thaxter certainly qualified.

When they were both nude, they kissed and fondled each other for long moments by the dim light of the oil lamp on the bedside table. Longarm drew her into his arms and she molded her body to his. Trapped between them, the thick shaft of his manhood prodded the softness of her belly.

They were still wrapped up in each other when they lowered themselves onto the bed. This cow town hotel room was hardly a palace, and the sheets, while clean, were a little coarse. The mattress had seen less lumpy days. There were a few flyspecks on the mirror over the dressing table.

Neither Longarm nor Caroline cared about the surroundings. All that mattered to them was that they were together. To Longarm, it was a bittersweet feeling, because he knew this might be the last time.

He stretched out on his back, and Caroline swung around and straddled him, facing away from him. That allowed her to lean over and take the head of his organ in her mouth. She held on to the shaft with both hands as she began running her tongue around the crown. Longarm groaned softly in pleasure as the tip of Caroline's tongue teased the sensitive slit.

For long moments he luxuriated in the oral pleasure she was bestowing on him, but then he started to feel guilty that he wasn't returning the favor. The way she was situated, her nether region with its twin openings was right there in front of his face. He slipped a finger into the tighter passage and ran his tongue along the damp, fleshy folds of the other.

That made Caroline lift her head long enough to gasp, "Oh, my God!" Then she bent to her chosen task with renewed energy, opening her mouth as wide as she could to engulf as much of him as possible. She sucked hard on him.

Longarm's tongue speared inside her again and again. Her hips quivered and jerked. They were working each other up closer and closer to culmination.

Suddenly Caroline lifted her head again, and although Longarm felt a twinge of disappointment, he knew somehow it wasn't going to last long. Caroline slid off him and positioned herself on hands and knees with her head near the foot of the bed. Her beautiful, sensuously curved rump stuck up enticingly in the air.

"Take me from behind, Custis!" she demanded in a breathless voice. "Take me now!"

Longarm thought that was a fine idea. He moved behind her and knelt so that the long, thick pole of flesh jutting out from his groin was lined up with her sex. For a second he regarded the puckered aperture between the cheeks of her rump with interest—some ladies had an uncommon fondness for doing it that way—but he decided to stick to the tried-and-true. The other was something that had to be discussed beforehand, elsewise somebody might be in for one hell of a surprise.

With a powerful thrust of his hips, he entered her. She gasped and clutched at the sheets with both hands. From this angle he could achieve a deep penetration, so he clutched her hips and drove into her as far as he could.

"My God, Custis!" she said. "You . . . you fill me up!"

With slow, forceful strokes, he slid in and out of her. She had been wet to start with, but under his steady lovemaking, she grew absolutely drenched. The soft, liquid sounds of their coupling provided accompaniment to the quiet gasps and groans that came from both of them as they scaled the heights of passion.

Unable to stand it any longer, Caroline shuddered and began to buck back against Longarm. He plunged into her a couple more times and then spasmed, flooding her with his hot juices. The moment was long and intense, strong enough to shake both of them to the core.

Though for a time that moment seemed endless, finally both of them were sated. Weakly, they slumped down, Caroline on her belly, Longarm on top of her with his member still buried inside her as it gradually softened. He supported most of his weight on hands and knees so that he wouldn't crush her, but they were still pressed together enough so that the skin-to-skin contact was highly enjoyable.

"My word, Custis," Caroline said after a while, "you seemed to put a little something extra into it that time!"

"I reckon you inspire the best in me," he told her.

In reality, he knew that this encounter might be their last. That was what had inspired him. He didn't want to tell her that . . . but it would be cowardly not to do so.

Sure, he could ride out early in the morning, before she was awake, and be miles away before she knew what was going on. But it wasn't his way to do such a thing, so he said now, "Caroline . . . there's something we need to talk about."

She turned her head and tried to look up at him, but couldn't quite do it. "What? What do you mean, Custis? Let me up, please."

He pulled out of her at last and sat back on his haunches. She rolled over and turned to face him, sitting cross-legged on the bed. That was a pretty revealing position, considering that she was naked as a jaybird, just like him, but he tried not to let his attention stray to what was between her legs at the base of that russet triangle.

"What is it, Custis?" she asked. "What's wrong?"

"Something's come up—"

Her eyes dropped to *his* groin.

"No, not that," he said hastily, "although if you look at it for too long, it might. What I'm talking about is something back in Lodestone."

Caroline frowned and repeated, "Back in Lodestone? I don't understand. I thought we were through with the place."

"So did I."

"Do you mean we'll have to go back and testify against that awful Riley Bascomb and his friend? I suppose I can do that if I need to."

"No, I reckon we can give sworn statements to the deputy before we leave. I'll work all that out. What I mean is that you'll be leaving on that train in a couple of days by yourself. I have to ride back over there."

Caroline's green eyes widened in surprise. "Why? I thought your case was over. The man you were after is dead and buried, remember?" An idea occurred to her. "Custis, have you figured out where Hathaway hid that stolen army payroll you were looking for?"

"Nope," he replied with a shake of his head, "but there may still be a way to track it down after all."

"How are you going to do that? Like I just said, Hathaway is dead."

"Maybe," Longarm said, "but there's a chance he's still alive."

He didn't add the other thought that had sprung into his mind as he looked at those reward dodgers on the deputy's desk.

Gordon Thaxter, the man Caroline had been searching for all these years, might still be alive, too . . .

Chapter 17

"Here's the reason I can't let it rest," Longarm said. He had gotten dressed again, but Caroline still sat on the bed with just a sheet wrapped around her. "I told Marshal Flynn what Hathaway looked like, and Flynn said he was dead and buried in the Lodestone cemetery. Flynn recognized him from *my* description, not the other way around."

Caroline shook her head. "I don't see how that means anything."

"It means Flynn might've been lying to me," Longarm said bluntly.

Caroline's frown deepened. "Why would he do that? He seemed like a good man, a good lawman."

"Seemed like it, all right," Longarm agreed. "But even a good man can be tempted. Say Hathaway came into town and wasn't sick at all. Maybe Flynn recognized him and tried to arrest him, maybe even got the drop on him." Longarm slid a cheroot out of his shirt pocket and put it between his lips. He left it unlit, and as his teeth clenched on it, he went on, "And then Hathaway offered the marshal a share of that payroll to let him go."

"Well . . . I suppose it could have happened like that. But why go to all the trouble of lying about him being sick, and pretending to bury him under another name?"

"Hathaway was a pretty smart hombre. He knew that I was after him, and he knew his own gang would be on his trail, too, after he double-crossed them in Junction City. More than likely he was more worried about them catching up to him than he was about me. He probably figured there was a good chance they'd kill me. They came close, too."

Understanding began to dawn in Caroline's eyes. "So Hathaway didn't offer to pay off Marshal Flynn just to let him go . . . He wanted to cover his trail, too, and make it look like he was dead."

Longarm nodded. "It could've happened that way. Hathaway leaves a chunk of that stolen loot with Flynn and then rides on, after arranging things with Flynn so that if anybody shows up looking for him, Flynn will pretend to recognize the description and show whoever it is the grave. That way, the trail ends in Lodestone, and whether it was me or those other outlaws, either of us'd be out of luck when it came to finding the payroll. Anybody looking for it would have to just turn around and ride away." Longarm's jaw tightened until he almost bit through the cheroot. "And all the while, Hathaway is on down the road somewhere laughing about how slick he is."

For a long moment, Caroline sat on the bed thinking over everything Longarm had said. Finally, she said, "It's an interesting idea, Custis, but . . . you can't prove any of it."

"No, I can't," Longarm agreed. "Not without looking in the grave of the so-called Calvin Johnson."

Caroline caught her breath, and he saw horror lurking in her eyes. "You'd dig up a grave?" she asked slowly.

"It ain't a chore I'm looking forward to," he admitted. "But it would prove, one way or another, whether my idea was right."

"Yes, it would. But if you *are* right, won't Marshal Flynn try to stop you? If Hathaway's not really buried there, then the marshal must have turned crooked."

"I don't like to think about a lawman going bad," Longarm said, "but it happens sometimes. And yeah, Flynn would probably try to stop me from digging up that grave . . . if he knew what I was going to do."

"So you're not going to tell him?"

Longarm shook his head. "Nope. I plan to get back to Lodestone without anybody knowing I'm there. If I open up that coffin and Nate Hathaway's really inside it, then I'll know I was wrong. If he ain't—"

"You'll confront Marshal Flynn then."

"That's right."

She thought it over for a moment and then nodded decisively. "I'm going with you."

"No, you're going to get on that train the day after tomorrow and go home," said Longarm. "There's no reason for you to go back to Lodestone. This is my job, not yours."

She scooted closer to the edge of the bed. "But Custis—"

"But me no buts," he said flatly. "If Flynn's trying to cover up Hathaway's getaway, I'll have to arrest him. There might be trouble. Gun trouble."

Caroline sighed. "And I suppose you don't need anything else to worry about, like me tagging along with you."

"To be blunt about it . . . that's right."

"I understand," she said grudgingly. Then she looked up hopefully. "But I could wait here for you—"

Longarm broke in. "I thought about that. Problem is, I may not be riding back this way at all. If Hathaway's not really dead, then I'll have to try to pick up his trail again. No telling which way I'll be heading from Lodestone."

"That's right," she admitted. "Damn it, Custis! I was looking forward to spending some more time with you."

He smiled. "I was looking forward to that, too. But sometimes this danged job of mine just won't let me do what I want."

"No, I suppose not. I guess you'll be leaving early in the morning?"

"Yep."

She lowered the sheet a little, so that the coral-tipped

swells of her breasts came into view. "And you need a good night's sleep."

He rubbed his jaw. "Well . . ."

The sheet drooped lower. "So it's unlikely that I could tempt you into staying a little while longer with me tonight."

He set the unlit cheroot on the night table and reached for the buttons of his shirt. "There's all kinds of things in the world that are unlikely," he said, "but that don't mean they're impossible . . ."

It was true that Longarm could have used some more sleep that night, but he was glad for the opportunity to keep Caroline distracted. He had told her just enough of the theory that had formed in his mind without going into the rest of it. But he didn't want her figuring out all the implications of everything he had said, either.

After a while he just gave up and spent the rest of the night in her room, then slipped out early the next morning before dawn, while she was still asleep. No one was in the hall to see him coming out of her door. He retrieved his gear from the room he had rented but hadn't used otherwise, and then went downstairs, confident that Caroline was still slumbering soundly.

It was so early that the hotel dining room wasn't open yet, but a hash house down the street was, and Longarm enjoyed a surprisingly good meal prepared by the proprietor, a burly black man who told Longarm that he'd been a cowboy until a bull broke his leg and the fracture hadn't healed right. That misfortune was a hungry man's gain, because the man's flapjacks were excellent and his coffee was almost as good.

Feeling refreshed and replenished, if not really rested, Longarm went to the livery stable and reclaimed his horse from a sleepy-eyed hostler. The deputy sheriff's office was locked up, so Longarm scribbled a note for Duncan and shoved it under the door. The note asked the deputy to continue holding Riley Bascomb and Cole and said that he would be in touch later.

Longarm's last stop was the train station, which was also the location of the telegraph office. The operator was sleepy, too, but he was awake enough to send off the telegrams Longarm wrote to the sheriffs of the next two counties over, as well as a wire addressed to Billy Vail in Denver explaining the situation. If Longarm knew his boss—and he'd been riding for Billy for a lot of years—Vail would burn up the telegraph lines between Colorado and Texas, making sure that the local authorities cooperated. Vail's years of service as a Texas Ranger still gave him a lot of influence in the Lone Star State.

Finally, Longarm was ready to ride out. The sun still wasn't up yet, but the eastern sky was orange and gold and pink with the approach of dawn.

It was pretty enough to make a fella wish he wasn't on his way to dig up a grave.

Longarm rode steadily all day, stopping only to rest his horse and stretch his legs every now and then. He ate his lunch in the saddle and washed it down with water from his canteen. Since he knew the way to Lodestone, he was able to make good time. By the end of the day he had covered more than half the distance.

That created a bit of a problem, because he wanted to approach the settlement after dark. The next day he took it easier, dawdling along and not pushing his mount at all. This was the day the train carrying Caroline was supposed to leave Trickham. He hoped she had gotten on her way without any trouble.

Late in the afternoon, while he was still several miles from Lodestone, he stopped and fixed himself a good supper, putting out the fire about the same time as the sun went down. Then he sat with his back against a tree, smoking contentedly, as he waited for the shadows to gather and for dusk to gradually turn into night.

Only when it was full dark did he mount up and ride on.

The two days in the saddle had given Longarm plenty of time to think about everything that had happened, everything he had seen and heard, and the theory that had grown up in his mind because of it. He was more convinced than ever that something fishy was going on in Lodestone. He didn't have all the details pinned down yet, of course—but he hoped to remedy that situation soon.

When the lights of the settlement appeared in front of him, he left the trail and swung his mount to the north, circling around so that he could approach the cemetery without riding through the town. Lodestone appeared to be peaceful and quiet. One time he barely caught the faint tinkle of piano music coming from one of the saloons. Other than that, the night was silent, except for the hoofbeats of Longarm's horse.

He reined in and dismounted when the dark bulk of the wooded hill behind the cemetery loomed above him. The hill was a forbidding mass, and Longarm felt a little tingle of some sort as he glanced at it, as if something evil lurked up there.

He didn't have time for that now, because he was pretty damned sure something evil lurked in the graveyard, and he had to investigate that first.

After tying his horse's reins to a tree, he moved forward stealthily until he came to the low stone wall that ran all around the cemetery. Longarm needed only a moment to climb over that wall and drop to the ground inside it. He paused there to listen and look around.

The cemetery was as silent as . . . well, as silent as the grave, he thought. No lights burned anywhere. Trees stood here and there, casting thick shadows on the ground. The moon had not yet risen, so only starlight played over the scene, and the illumination it provided was faint.

There was enough light, though, for Longarm to be able to see the tombstones lined up in neat rows. Some were small and simple, others larger and more ornate.

From his previous visit, Longarm recalled that there was a small shed just inside the grounds, near the gate. The hulking Lonnie, Edgar Horne's assistant at the undertaking parlor, served as the caretaker of the cemetery as well, and Longarm suspected that he would find Lonnie's shovel inside that shed. Trying not to step on any of the graves, he circled through the cemetery toward the entrance.

He could see the church at the bottom of the hill, its whitewashed sides easily visible even in the darkness. The church itself was as dark and quiet as the cemetery. The preacher had gone home for the night. Nobody had any reason to be poking around up here.

Nobody except a lawman looking for some particularly tricky owlhoots.

He reached the shed. The door had a simple latch, without any sort of lock. Obviously, Lonnie wasn't worried about thieves. Quietly, Longarm lifted the latch and eased the door open. The hinges squealed a little, but not much.

Something about stepping into that darkness made Longarm's nerves tighten. Prairie dogs skittered up and down his spine. But he didn't want to show a light, just in case anybody happened to be looking up here, so he moved forward into the shed before he used his thumbnail to light the lucifer that he held in his left hand.

Squinting his eyes against the sudden flare of the match, Longarm looked around and saw that the shed was empty except for a wheelbarrow, a pair of lanterns, a couple of shovels, a rake, and a scythe that Lonnie no doubt used to keep weeds from growing up inside the graveyard. Longarm picked up one of the shovels and then dropped the match and ground it out under his heel.

His nerves weren't quite as taut as he left the shed and started making his way toward the spot where "Calvin Johnson" was supposedly buried. Longarm thought it was entirely possible there was nobody in the coffin at all. He felt anticipation growing inside him. He was eager to find out if his theory was right. There were other things here that he wanted to check on, too, but determining the fate of Nate Hathaway came first.

He told himself that it was only natural a fella would get a mite spooked, tramping around a graveyard after dark. Even in the hardiest of souls, there always lurked a touch of fear about what lay on the other side of death. When he crossed that great divide, each man was a pioneer, going where he had never gone before.

Longarm pushed those thoughts out of his head and concentrated on the task at hand. He found the grave he was looking for, and just to make sure he had the right one, he ran his fingertips over the name etched into the marker. "CALVIN JOHNSON," it read. Even though Longarm had told Marshal Flynn that it was really Nate Hathaway who was buried here, the tombstone hadn't been changed.

Maybe that was appropriate, considering what Longarm expected to find when he opened up the coffin.

Carefully, he pushed the blade of the shovel into the ground. Even though this earth had been turned recently, enough time had passed so that the digging wasn't easy. Longarm tossed several shovelfuls of dirt to the side and felt beads of sweat break out on his forehead.

The sounds of his digging almost covered up the faint scrape of boot leather on the ground behind him. But Longarm's keen hearing picked it up and warned him. Moving swiftly, he swung around, the shovel still clutched in his hands.

And froze as he saw the terrifying figure looming there, scythe in hand, the Grim Reaper come to deal out harsh punishment to one who had been foolish enough to venture into his domain.

Chapter 18

The shocking tableau lasted only a heartbeat. Then the massive figure leaped forward, swinging the scythe and shouting in a harsh voice, "Get outta my graveyard!"

Instinctively, Longarm lifted the shovel and parried the scythe with it before the glittering blade could slice into his flesh. The impact as scythe and shovel blade clanged together shivered through Longarm's hands, but he managed to hold on to the shovel. He twisted aside, out of the path of the big man's charge, and jabbed the shovel handle into Lonnie's stomach. Lonnie didn't even slow down.

Longarm had realized almost immediately that it was the cemetery caretaker who confronted him, not some spectral collector of souls. Lonnie was still mighty dangerous, though, even if he wasn't the Grim Reaper. He chopped and slashed at Longarm with the scythe, and the lawman was forced to back up hastily as he fended off the savage attack.

Longarm recalled that one time when he'd been visiting the vast Circle Star Ranch in South Texas owned by his friend Jessica Starbuck, Jessie's half-American, half-Japanese protector and sidekick Ki had shown him how to use the Japanese fighting staff known as a *bo*. He put his memories of that practice session to good use now as he twirled the shovel and rapped the handle against Lonnie's head. The thick-skulled galoot seemed to shake off the blow right away, though. Longarm ducked aside from a downward stroke of the scythe and whipped the shovel handle across Lonnie's face, aiming for the nose. The blow landed with a satisfying *whap*!

Lonnie howled in pain and staggered a couple of steps to the side. That gave Longarm the time he needed to drop the shovel and pull the Colt from the cross-draw rig on his left hip. He leveled the gun at the caretaker and said, "Hold it, Lonnie! I don't want to shoot you, old son, but I will if I have to!"

Longarm didn't know if Lonnie was actually feebleminded or just a little slow. Clearly, though, Lonnie regarded the Lodestone cemetery as his territory and didn't want any interlopers messing around in it, especially after dark. Nor did Longarm know how Lonnie had spotted him up here, but that didn't matter now. The only important thing was for him to get through to Lonnie and put a stop to this fight before someone was badly hurt.

Lonnie held the scythe in his left hand and raised his right to his nose, which was streaming blood. Longarm could see the dark flow, even in the faint light from the stars.

"You broke my nose," Lonnie said thickly.

"Sorry," said Longarm. "It was that or let you carve me up into little pieces, and I didn't cotton to that idea."

"You're in the graveyard, and you broke my nose. You shouldn't be here. You shouldn't'a hurt me."

"Damn it, Lonnie, I've got a gun on you—" Longarm began.

Lonnie ignored the warning, and with a roar of rage, he flung the scythe at Longarm. The lawman was forced to throw himself to the ground as the deadly tool spun through the air toward him at blinding speed.

Still bellowing furiously, Lonnie charged right behind

the scythe. Longarm tipped the barrel of the Colt up and fired, but he didn't know if the shot struck his opponent. Lonnie certainly didn't slow down. Instead, his foot lashed out in a kick, connected with Longarm's hand, and sent the gun flying off into the darkness.

Longarm bit back a curse as he rolled to the side, cradling his throbbing hand against his body. Lonnie slammed down on the ground where Longarm had been a second earlier. If the giant had landed on him, Longarm would have been pinned down and had the breath knocked out of him, at the very least. More than likely he would have suffered some broken ribs.

As it was, though, he was still in the fight, even though now the situation looked more bleak than ever as Longarm scrambled to his feet. Big he might be, but Lonnie was even bigger. And now Longarm was unarmed except for his derringer, and he wasn't sure the little gun would have any effect on Lonnie.

The only advantage Longarm had was in speed. Lonnie wasn't really slow, but his muscle-bound stature made his movements a bit more lumbering than Longarm's were. When Lonnie climbed to his feet and charged again, swinging his fists, Longarm was able to dart aside. As Lonnie went past him, he clubbed his hands together and smashed them against the back of the caretaker's neck.

The heavy blow staggered Lonnie but didn't put him down. He swiped backhanded at Longarm with an arm that was like the trunk of a small tree. Longarm ducked under it, stepped in, and pistoned a hard right and left into Lonnie's kidneys. That smacked of dirty fighting, but Longarm knew he was in a battle for his life and couldn't afford any niceties.

As Lonnie grunted in pain, Longarm stuck a foot between his ankles and rammed a shoulder into his back. Lonnie lost his balance and went down, crashing to the ground. Longarm leaped on him and jabbed a knee savagely into the small of Lonnie's back. At the same time he grabbed Lonnie's head, twisting his fingers in the thick mop of dark hair. Using that grip, Longarm smashed Lonnie's face against the ground, dealing out that much more punishment to the already bleeding and probably broken nose.

Lonnie whimpered this time, like an animal caught in a trap, but Longarm didn't allow himself to feel sorry for the brutish caretaker. He slammed Lonnie's face into the ground again and again until finally the huge man went limp. His breath made a harsh bubbling sound as air rasped through the damaged nose.

Breathing heavily himself, Longarm pushed himself up and off of his stunned opponent. He had lost his hat, his gun, and the shovel he had been using to dig up the so-called grave of Nate Hathaway. As he turned to look for them, he saw that another figure had entered the cemetery. The newcomer stood about ten feet away, and starlight gleamed off the barrel of the gun he pointed at Longarm.

"Don't move, mister," the man snapped, "except to lift those hands where I can see 'em!"

Longarm recognized the voice. It belonged to Marshal Artemus Flynn. He hadn't wanted Flynn to know he was back in Lodestone until after he had checked out the suspicious grave and a few other things, but now that plan was ruined. Lonnie's arrival had seen to that.

"Take it easy, Marshal," Longarm said as he lifted his hands. "It's just me, Custis Long."

"Marshal Long?" Flynn sounded shocked. He lowered his gun somewhat but kept it pointing in Longarm's general direction. "What are you doing here? I thought you'd be halfway back to Denver by now." A note of anger came into Flynn's voice. "And what do you think you're doing, beating the hell out of poor Lonnie like that?"

"Poor Lonnie damn near beat the hell out of me," replied Longarm, letting some irritation creep into his own voice. "Not only that, he took a scythe to me and came mighty close to chopping me into pieces!"

"Well, I reckon he didn't know who you were. He's very protective of this cemetery. He doesn't like anybody messing around in it."

Longarm glanced at the motionless figure on the ground. "I got that idea. But he never stopped to ask who I was or what I was doing here. He just came after me, and I had to defend myself."

"What *are* you doing here?" Flynn asked, and Longarm was reminded of the fact that he suspected the marshal of being crooked. Flynn had his gun drawn, too, and Longarm's Colt was still lying somewhere on the ground.

He had to play his cards close to the vest, he warned himself. "I just came back to follow up on something," he said. "I got to worrying that my boss wouldn't be satisfied with my report if I couldn't tell him that I'd seen Nate Hathaway's body with my own eyes."

Longarm wanted to keep Flynn's attention focused on the Hathaway case. That was enough to deal with for right now.

Distaste was evident in Flynn's voice as he said, "So you snuck back into Lodestone and decided to dig up a grave?"

Longarm wished folks would stop saying that, even though it was accurate. It made him feel like some sort of ghoul.

"I just thought I'd take a look inside that coffin, so I could tell Chief Marshal Vail that Hathaway is really buried there. Then I figured I'd ride on. Didn't see any need to bother anybody with this."

He watched Flynn closely. If the local lawman was crooked, he couldn't let Longarm look inside the coffin. Longarm had spotted the shovel lying on the ground nearby. If Flynn looked like he was going to take a shot at him, Longarm was going to make a try for that shovel. He could grab it and fling it at Flynn, maybe throw off the marshal's aim . . .

"Oh, for God's sake," Flynn said disgustedly. "If that's all you wanted, you should have just come to me and told me. You didn't have to skulk around and nearly kill a poor dumb fella who's never hurt a soul in his life."

Longarm couldn't help but stare. Flynn still sounded mighty annoyed, but he didn't act like a man who had something criminal to hide. In fact, the marshal lowered the hammer on his gun and then slipped the revolver back into its holster.

"When I was making my rounds and heard all the yelling up here, I didn't know what to make of it," Flynn went on, "so I thought I'd better come have a look. I sure didn't expect to find something like this going on." He walked over to the shovel, bent to pick it up, and held it out toward Longarm. "Here."

Longarm took the shovel. With a frown, he said, "You want me to . . . ?"

Flynn waved toward Hathaway's grave. "Go ahead. Help yourself, Marshal. If you want to dig him up, then by all means dig him up." Flynn paused. "Just don't expect me to help you. I'm going to see to Lonnie. I hope you didn't hurt him too bad."

Longarm gritted his teeth at the scornful tone in Flynn's voice. He was irritated by the marshal's attitude, but he was also beginning to worry that his theory had been all wrong. If there was anything in that grave Flynn wanted to hide, surely he wouldn't be telling Longarm to dig it up.

Flynn went over to Lonnie, rolled him onto his back with a grunt of effort, and started trying to revive him. Meanwhile, Longarm looked around until he spotted his Colt lying on top of a grave. He picked it up and holstered it. Flynn paid no attention to him.

Longarm walked over to the spot where he had been digging before Lonnie interrupted him. He put the shovel blade against the earth, rested his foot on it, and pushed. The shovel went into the ground. Longarm lifted it and tossed the dirt to the side.

He had dug plenty of graves in his life; more than enough, in fact. It wasn't an easy task. At least this time he didn't have to go down all the way, just far enough so that he uncovered the lid of the coffin. His muscles began to ache as he worked steadily.

Meanwhile, Lonnie had come around, and Marshal Flynn raised him to a sitting position. Longarm could see them and hear the conversation as Flynn asked what had happened.

"I was sleepin' around behind the shed, like I always do when the weather's nice," Lonnie rumbled. "I heard a little noise and got up and come around the shed in time to see a fella walkin' away from it with one o' my shovels. I figured he was stealin' it, and I wouldn'ta cared so much about that, but then he come up here and started diggin' up a grave. I couldn't let him dig up no grave, Marshal. It wouldn't be right."

Flynn patted him on the shoulder and said gently, "No, Lonnie, I reckon you couldn't. Nobody needs to be digging in this graveyard except you."

Lonnie nodded his shaggy head, and Longarm felt a twinge of guilt. This whole evening sure wasn't working out the way he had hoped it would.

Lonnie wiped blood away from his nose and then pointed with his gore-smeared hand. "But he's over there now, diggin'," he protested. "That ain't right, Marshal."

"No, no, it's all right this time," Flynn explained. "I told him to dig up that grave."

"Nobody's supposed to dig up a grave once a body's in the ground!" Lonnie sounded horrified by the very idea.

"I know," Flynn said to soothe him. "This is different, though. This is the only time it'll ever happen."

"Better be," Lonnie mumbled.

Longarm was down a good ways by now. He plunged the shovel into the dirt again and felt the blade hit something solid. It made a scraping sound.

Flynn heard the noise, too, and must have known what it

meant. He patted Lonnie on the shoulder again and said, "You just sit right here for a few minutes, if you're all right. Then I'll take you down to see Doc Donaldson and make sure you're not hurt bad."

"I'm fine, Marshal," Lonnie said. "My nose just hurts a mite."

"Well, we'll get it tended to." Flynn stood up and walked toward the grave where Longarm was working.

"Sounds like you're almost there, Marshal," he said.

Longarm grunted. "A few more minutes and I'll have it."

"I hope you know you're going to feel like a damn fool when you open it up."

"We'll see," Longarm said. He had come too far to stop now, no matter what he found in that coffin when he lifted the lid.

While Longarm finished clearing away the dirt from the top of the coffin, Flynn walked down to the shed and came back with one of the lanterns. He struck a match and lit the wick. The glow from the lantern washed over the ugly hole in the earth Longarm had created.

Longarm's shirt was drenched in sweat now. He stopped, leaned on the shovel handle for a moment, and sleeved moisture from his forehead. The narrow lid of the coffin was visible, and he had dug out around it enough so that he could hunker beside it. As he did so, Flynn moved to the foot of the grave and held the lantern higher so that it shone brightly on the coffin.

"All right, Marshal," he said. "Go ahead and take the lid off. Let's see what you've found."

Longarm glanced up, and saw that Flynn had the lantern in his left hand while his right rested on the butt of his gun. It occurred to him suddenly that if the coffin *was* empty, all it would take to fill it would be one quick shot.

Then Flynn could shovel all the dirt back into the hole, and no one other than him and Lonnie would ever know that a federal lawman had come snooping around the Lodestone cemetery.

If Flynn tried to make such a play, Longarm would be ready for it and would match his gun speed against the other man's. It sure as hell wouldn't be the first time . . .

He got the tip of the shovel blade under the coffin lid and began levering it up. The nails resisted, of course, and Longarm had to heave hard on the shovel before the nails let go with an unnerving screech of metal against wood. Longarm recoiled involuntarily as an unmistakable smell wafted up from inside the pine box.

Somebody was in there, that was for sure.

"Lift it," Flynn grated.

Longarm dropped the shovel, grasped the lid, and wrenched it up and off the coffin. During the storm a few days earlier, water had run in and hastened the decomposition process. Longarm had seen a lot of ugly things in his life, but few of them had been any uglier than the face that stared sightlessly up at him from inside the coffin.

The face was one he knew, having seen it a little over a week earlier in Junction City. Even in the state it was in now, he recognized it.

It belonged to Nate Hathaway.

Chapter 19

"Satisfied?" Marshal Flynn asked.

Slowly, Longarm lowered the lid back onto the coffin, glad to be covering up what he had seen there. Thoughts whirled through his brain, but he carefully kept his face impassive as he lined up the nails and began tapping them back down with the shovel. It was an awkward task, but he got it done.

"Did you really think Hathaway wouldn't be in there?"

"Like I told you, Marshal," Longarm said, "I had to see it with my own eyes."

"Well, now you have. I'll ask you to cover this grave up again while I take Lonnie to see the doctor."

Longarm nodded as he finished with the last nail. "Sure." He forced himself to add, "Tell him I'm sorry for what happened."

He wasn't all that sorry, because every instinct in his body still told him that something was wrong here. But he wanted Flynn to leave, so he pretended to cooperate and be remorseful about the fight with the caretaker.

"Want me to leave the lantern?" asked Flynn.

"If you wouldn't mind, that'd be a help."

"Sure." Flynn set the lantern on the ground beside the

open grave. "Why don't you come by my office when you get through up here?"

"I'll do that," Longarm promised. He might have some questions he wanted answered.

As Longarm climbed out of the hole in the ground, Flynn went over to Lonnie and helped him up. Lonnie glared at Longarm but allowed Flynn to lead him away. They headed for the cemetery entrance, Lonnie shambling along beside the local lawman and holding his battered nose.

Shoveling the dirt back into the grave went faster than taking it out. By the light of the lantern, Longarm worked steadily until the earth was mounded up again in front of the marker with its false inscription. He wondered if anybody would ever get around to changing it to reflect the true identity of the grave's occupant.

With that done, he picked up the lantern. It was going to make the rest of his job easier. Flynn and Lonnie were gone now, and Longarm was alone in the cemetery.

Alone with the dead . . .

After finding his hat, he walked along the rows of graves, holding the lantern up so that he could read the names on the markers. As in any small town cemetery, most of the tombstones had birth and death dates inscribed on them along with the occasional flowery sentiment, and many of the people buried here had been elderly when they died. But there were some younger people, too, and a few children and infants.

Longarm's jaw tightened when he saw those markers. Almost more than anything, he hated the idea of a youngster's life being cut short. It had always seemed mighty unfair to him, and the words of the old hymn were scant comfort. As the song said, farther along we might know more about it, but it still didn't seem right.

He had work to do, though, so he forced himself to concentrate on that. Once, as the light from the lantern suddenly spilled over a tall, threatening figure, he tensed and started to reach for his gun before he realized that it wasn't a man standing there at the head of a grave, but rather the statue of an angel. Longarm grimaced and moved on.

There was one of the graves he was looking for. He paused in front of it. This marker had only a name—Roy Burke—and the date of death inscribed on it. Burke had died six months earlier.

In the next row he found a similar marker. Evidently Clyde Williams hadn't been anybody's beloved son, father, or husband. He just got a name and death date, too.

In the next quarter of an hour, Longarm found four more graves like that, belonging to Ben Culbertson, John Edward Traft, William Hargett, and Tom Shefford. There might be others like that in the cemetery, but that was enough to satisfy Longarm. When he had left the grave-yard several days earlier with Caroline and Marshal Flynn, he had read the names on most of the markers they passed, without really thinking about it. As a matter of habit, those names had stuck in his brain. Remembering things was something that a good lawman just did automatically.

So a couple of days later, when he stood in front of the deputy sheriff's desk in Trickham and saw some of those same names on the wanted posters scattered in front of Duncan, he recognized them. His thoughts had leaped from those reward dodgers to these gravestones. Evidently, Nate Hathaway and Gordon Thaxter weren't the only wanted men to have died and been buried in Lodestone.

A part of him wanted to use the shovel tucked under his arm and start digging again. He had done enough for to-night, though. Flynn had dismissed him as a damned fool, and he wanted the local marshal to keep thinking of him that way. Maybe Flynn really didn't know anything about what was going on here, but Longarm found that hard to believe, and he had already made Flynn suspicious enough of him.

There was the matter of Nate Hathaway, too. Hathaway was definitely dead and buried. Where did that fact fit in with the theory Longarm had worked out? He couldn't answer that question, so he thought it might be best to poke around some more and try to tie up that loose end.

Longarm was on his way out of the cemetery when he saw another fresh grave. He only had to go a short distance out of his way to check the marker.

He wasn't really surprised, but he still gave a little grunt of satisfaction when he saw the name Jack Meehan and the date from the day before.

After leaving the shovel and the lantern in the shed, Longarm walked the short distance down the hill and past the church to reach the main street of Lodestone. Lights burned in a few houses on the side streets, but the businesses were all dark except for the saloons and the marshal's office.

After everything that had happened, Longarm wouldn't have minded stopping at one of the saloons for a shot of Maryland rye. He postponed that pleasure and headed for Flynn's office instead.

When he got there, he didn't knock. He just grasped the knob and opened the door. As he stepped into the office he saw Flynn sitting behind the desk and noted that the local lawman wasn't alone. Mayor Hugh Bascomb sat stolidly in the chair in front of the desk. He turned toward Longarm a face that was dark with anger.

"There you are!" Bascomb said, looking like he was about ready to pop a blood vessel. "By God, sir, you are a sorry excuse for a lawman. Marshal Flynn tells me that now you've sunk to desecrating graves!"

"There wasn't any desecration going on," Longarm said, feeling annoyed that he had to defend himself against Bascomb's accusations. "I was just trying to do my job properly and make sure that the federal fugitive I was after was really dead."

"You could have come to me or Marshal Flynn or Coroner Horne and gotten permission to exhume the body. That would have been the proper way to do things."

Bascomb would have been right, of course—if not for the fact that Longarm had suspected Flynn was a crooked son of a bitch. It had been entirely possible, too—still was, as a matter of fact—that Bascomb and Horne were in on the scheme.

Longarm didn't want them to know the depth of his suspicions, though, so he just nodded and said ruefully, "I reckon you're right, Mayor."

Bascomb snorted disdainfully. "Of course I'm right."

Flynn seemed to have gotten over his anger. In a mild voice that sounded more like his normal tone, he said, "Did you take care of that grave, Marshal?"

"All covered up and patted down," Longarm assured him. "In a week or so you won't hardly be able to tell that it was ever dug up."

"Good. You may be interested to know that Lonnie does have a broken nose. Doc Donaldson is tending to it now."

Longarm grimaced. "Hope you'll tell him I'm sorry. I reckon he wouldn't much want to hear it directly from me."

"You can't blame him for holding a grudge. He's like a child."

"Whatever the doc's bill is, I'll take care of it," Longarm offered.

"Never mind about that," snapped Bascomb. "In his capacity as caretaker of the cemetery, Lonnie works for the town of Lodestone. We'll take care of his medical expenses. What I want to know is—where the hell is my son?"

Longarm raised his eyebrows in surprise. Seeing the reaction, Flynn said, "I asked Mayor Bascomb to come down to the office so that the two of you could talk. Riley's been missing for the past few days, and Hugh thought you might know something about it."

Longarm was on more solid footing now. This didn't involve some murky plot, the details of which were still somewhat unclear to him. He said, "Matter of fact, I do know where your boy is, Mayor."

Bascomb came to his feet. "By God, if you've hurt him—"

"He's all right," Longarm cut in. "Got a bullet graze on one leg, but that's all."

"You *shot* him?"

"Seemed like the thing to do at the time," drawled Longarm, "seeing as how he'd been doing his damnedest to shoot me."

"A lie!" Bascomb shouted. "Another damnable lie! Where is he? Where is my son?"

"Behind bars where he belongs. He's in the jail at Trickham."

"On what charge?" Bascomb demanded furiously.

"Charges." Longarm corrected him. "Attempted murder, for one, and kidnapping for another. You could probably throw in molesting a woman, too, even though he and his pards got stopped short of outright rape."

Bascomb blinked rapidly and opened and closed his mouth several times. Longarm wouldn't have thought it possible that the mayor could get any more red in the face, but Bascomb managed somehow.

Flynn came to his feet and looked upset, too. He said, "You'd better tell us about this, Marshal."

"Glad to." Longarm took out a cheroot, lit it, and blew smoke toward the ceiling, taking a little guilty pleasure in the way his deliberateness made Bascomb squirm. He went on, "Riley and two of his pards, a couple of cowboys named Cole and Bradford, followed Miss Thaxter and me and jumped us while we were camped between here and Trickham. They tried to kill me and thought that they had. They rode off with Miss Thaxter as their prisoner, with the intention of raping and probably killing her."

Bascomb finally found his voice again. "That's insane! Riley would never do such a thing!"

Longarm looked at him and said, "Do you really not

140

know your boy, or are you just plumb stupid, Mayor?" Without waiting for an answer, he continued the story. "I went after them and caught up to them before they could do more than terrorize Miss Thaxter. There was a ruckus. Bradford got killed. I arrested Riley and Cole and took them on to Trickham. Deputy Norm Duncan, who works for the Coleman County sheriff, locked them up in his jail pending them being officially charged."

"This isn't Coleman County," Flynn pointed out. "Sounds to me like there's a tricky little jurisdictional dispute involved."

"That's why I sent wires to the sheriffs of all the counties that might be involved," said Longarm. "They can work it out. Meanwhile, Riley's locked up so that he can't hurt anybody else."

Bascomb slammed a pudgy fist down on the marshal's desk. "I want you to ride back over there and get him released right now! You'll drop those false charges against him, if you know what's good for you!"

"The charges ain't false," Longarm said, "and I never have cottoned to folks trying to tell me what's good for me."

Bascomb turned to Flynn and pointed a shaking finger at Longarm. "Marshal, arrest that man!"

Flynn scratched at his ear and made an uncomfortable face. "On, uh, what charges, Mayor?"

"Charges? Charges? I don't care about the stinking charges! Just arrest him!" Bascomb sputtered and shook. "Destruction of public property, that'll do! He dug up a grave! Desecration! Blasphemy!"

"Well, blasphemy isn't really against state or local law," Flynn said. "It's more of a sin than a crime. And Long didn't really destroy or desecrate anything. He put the grave back like he found it. As close as he could, anyway."

"He admitted he shot Riley! You can lock him up for that!"

Flynn shook his head. "From the sound of it, the shooting was self-defense. Anyway, I didn't see the fracas myself, and we don't have any witnesses to swear that Marshal Long did anything illegal."

"Riley's your witness! Riley will swear that Long tried to murder him."

"Riley's in jail over at Trickham," Flynn pointed out. "He can't swear to anything here in Lodestone."

"Marshal, I'm ordering you—"

"I'm sorry, Mayor," Flynn said, and now his voice had taken on a hard edge. "Under the circumstances, I can't arrest Marshal Long."

Bascomb did that fishlike opening and closing of his mouth again. After a moment he turned to Longarm and said, "You'll be sorry. You'll be sorry you ever set foot in Lodestone."

Around the cheroot, Longarm said, "Could be I already am."

Bascomb just glared at him and stomped out of the marshal's office. Flynn shook his head as he watched the mayor go.

When the echo of the slamming door had faded, Flynn said, "Are you satisfied now that Nate Hathaway is really dead and buried, Marshal?"

"You were there when I opened the coffin," Longarm said. "I reckon I have to be."

"Then you don't have any reason to stay here in Lodestone, do you?"

"Are you telling me to get out of town tonight?" asked Longarm.

"No, I wouldn't run a man out of town in the middle of the night. First thing in the morning, though, I think it'd be a mighty good thing if you rode out and didn't come back. That way Lodestone can get back to being—"

"A peaceable town, I know. All right," Longarm agreed.

But he was stretching the truth, of course. He wasn't through with Lodestone just yet.

Not by a long shot.

Chapter 20

After fetching his horse from where he had tied it near the graveyard, and leaving the mount at the stable, Longarm went over to the hotel and got a room for the night. Stevens, the proprietor, looked surprised to see him. "I thought you had left town, Marshal," he commented.

"I did. Had to turn around and come back."

"Not more trouble, I hope. Lodestone has always been such a—"

Longarm held up a hand to stop him before he could say it. "Just give me the key."

Stevens looked offended, but he took a key off the rack and put it on the desk. "Is Miss Thaxter with you this time?" he asked coolly.

Longarm shook his head. "Nope. I'm alone."

"Very well. That's the same room you had before, you'll notice."

"Much obliged," Longarm said, although he didn't really care. He had left his saddle with the horse at Monklin's livery barn. Carrying his Winchester, he went up the stairs and unlocked the door of the room.

He had been thinking about how to proceed. He wanted to get another look at some of those graves in the cemetery,

143

but he suspicioned that Flynn might be keeping an eye on the place tonight. Flynn thought he had Longarm fooled, but he would be too careful to count on that. If he was smart enough to come up with the scheme in the first place, he would be smart enough to be worried about Longarm as long as the federal lawman was in town.

So Longarm got undressed, blew out the lamp, and with his Colt beside him, stretched out on the bed to smoke a cheroot and ponder the situation.

Although finding Nate Hathaway's corpse in that coffin had been unexpected, it didn't really invalidate Longarm's theory but rather just complicated it a mite. The broad outlines were still there and still made sense, but Longarm went over the theory again in his mind to be sure.

Obviously, things hadn't begun with Hathaway. For quite some time, wanted men had been coming to Lodestone, only to die and be buried here. But they hadn't died, of course, and their so-called graves had to be empty. Some outlaws would pay a considerable amount to get a fresh start and a guarantee that the law wouldn't continue looking for them. Nothing would accomplish that as well as being dead in the eyes of the world. And right there in the Lodestone cemetery were the tombstones to prove it.

The news that a man could "die" and be reborn with a new identity in Lodestone would travel fast along the owl-hoot trail. Whoever was in charge of the scheme could get rich, especially if he was patient and didn't charge too much for the service. Longarm was convinced that Bascomb hadn't come up with the idea; the mayor wasn't smart enough for that.

But Flynn was, or at least so Longarm's gut told him. The local undertaker would have to be in on the deal, too, and it was entirely possible that the doctor and the mayor knew about it as well. Even splitting the take four ways, over time the scheme would make them rich men. Longarm looked at it from every angle and was convinced that it was not only feasible, but also that he had stumbled onto the truth.

Problem was, he still didn't have any proof. An empty coffin where Nate Hathaway should have been would have done the job. But Hathaway's coffin hadn't been empty, and Longarm was left without any evidence.

He couldn't see any way around it.

He was going to have to dig up some more graves.

But not tonight. If he went up to the cemetery tonight, Flynn might be waiting for him. He had to make the local lawman think that he had gotten away with it—again.

So Longarm put his cigar out, rolled over, and went to sleep.

He wouldn't have been surprised if somebody had tried to kill him during the night. He had already started to wonder if it had been Marshal Flynn who had taken those shots at him in the bathhouse, rather than Riley Bascomb. Flynn's first reaction could have been that he didn't want a federal lawman poking around Lodestone.

Or maybe it *had* been Riley, as Longarm had first suspected. The bastard was certainly full of enough hate to have done such a thing. At this point, the identity of the bushwhacker didn't really matter.

Longarm slept lightly, as he always did when potential danger threatened. The night passed quietly, though, without any trouble, and he woke up in the morning feeling fairly well rested.

The trick now was to act as if everything was normal. He got dressed and went downstairs for breakfast in the hotel dining room. He smiled at Hannah the waitress and flirted with her a little, just as he would have if he didn't have a care in the world. He was lingering over a second cup of coffee when Marshal Flynn came into the dining room, spotted him, and walked over to the table.

"Morning, Marshal," Flynn said.

Longarm nodded and gestured toward the empty chair on the other side of the table. "Care to join me?" he asked.

"Don't mind if I do, but just for coffee. I ate already."

Flynn took off his hat and sat down. Longarm caught Hannah's eye, pointed at his cup, and then pointed to Flynn. She filled another cup from the pot, set it on a saucer, and brought it over.

"Thank you, Hannah," Flynn said.

"Put that on my bill," Longarm told her.

Flynn shrugged. "I won't argue with you. Obliged, Marshal."

Longarm smiled and said, "I reckon the biggest favor I can do for you, though, is to get out of town."

Flynn sipped his coffee and set the cup back on the saucer. It didn't rattle a bit. He was a mighty cool customer, thought Longarm.

"I believe that's what we agreed to," Flynn said. "Your presence here is very upsetting to Mayor Bascomb."

"He wouldn't have anything to be upset about if his boy wasn't such a troublemaking asshole."

Flynn looked like he didn't know whether to be angry or amused. He settled for another shrug and said, "I won't argue that point with you, either. Riley Bascomb is stupid, and his father isn't much brighter. But Hugh *is* the mayor."

"Which makes him your boss."

"In some respects."

This conversation was making Longarm more convinced than ever that Flynn was the architect of the scheme. Flynn kept it well hidden most of the time, but he had an arrogance about him, a sense that he considered himself smarter than just about everybody around him.

Before Longarm was through, though, Flynn would learn that it was possible to outsmart himself.

Longarm just hoped he wouldn't fall into that same trap.

"Don't worry, Marshal," he said. "Soon as I finish this

cup of coffee, I plan to get my horse and ride out. And this time I won't be coming back."

"No reason to, is there? You found Hathaway."

"No reason to at all," Longarm agreed. "My job here is done." He couldn't resist adding, "Last night I noticed another fresh grave up there in the cemetery. Somebody else die recent-like?"

Flynn nodded solemnly. "Yeah, day before yesterday, in fact. Just a drifter on his way through town. He stopped for a drink and made the mistake of walking behind a bad horse. Got kicked in the head for his trouble. Stove his skull right in."

Longarm made a clucking sound and shook his head. "Damned shame. You know who he was?"

"Papers on him gave his name as Jack Meehan. Why? Do you know him?"

"Never heard of him before," Longarm said. "I just wanted to point out that I was nowhere around when it happened, so that so-called jinx you accused me of carrying with me couldn't have had anything to do with it."

Flynn chuckled. "No, I suppose not. Still . . ."

"You'll be glad to see me go."

As if toasting Longarm, Flynn just lifted his coffee cup and smiled.

The big lawman drained the last of his own coffee and then stood. "I'll settle up with Stevens, and then I'll be gone, Marshal."

"So long," Flynn said.

Longarm put on his hat, nodded, and left the dining room without looking back.

He paid for his room and the meal, including Flynn's cup of coffee, and then went down to the stable to get his horse. By the time the mount was saddled and ready to ride, Flynn had stepped out onto the porch of the hotel. He leaned a shoulder against one of the posts holding up the porch roof and watched as Longarm rode out of town. Longarm was aware of Flynn watching him, but he didn't give any sign that he noticed the local lawman's scrutiny.

Question now was whether or not Flynn would follow him to make sure that he didn't double back.

Longarm kept an eye on the trail behind him all morning and didn't see any sign of anyone tracking him. If Flynn was back there, he was as tricky as an Indian. By the middle of the day, Longarm had decided that Flynn had accepted his act. Longarm's return to Lodestone had been a brief setback for Flynn, but the local lawman, smart son of a bitch that he was, believed he had put one over on the dumb federal star packer.

And now that dumb federal star packer was ready to turn around and show Flynn just how wrong he was.

Longarm reined his horse off the trail, rode up onto a brushy knoll, and found a good place to wait. He sat there for a couple of hours, just to make sure that Flynn or somebody else from Lodestone wasn't going to show up. Finally, around the middle of the afternoon, Longarm started back the way he had come from. Once again, he was going to time his arrival in Lodestone for after night had fallen.

Just as he had the night before, he circled around the settlement when he reached it. It was possible Flynn might be guarding the cemetery again tonight, but Longarm considered that unlikely. As far as Flynn knew, he had pulled the wool over Longarm's eyes. Still, Longarm would be careful and approach the cemetery from the rear.

He was later tonight, which meant that even more of the townspeople had already turned in. Lodestone was mostly dark when Longarm paused on the hillside above the little valley and looked down on the town.

As he dismounted, the wind picked up, sighing through the trees and rattling their branches. The tang that the wind carried told Longarm there was a storm somewhere not far off. He could smell the rain. The low rumble of thunder that sounded a moment later came as no surprise.

He left the horse tied in the woods on the hillside and

148

walked toward the stone fence around the cemetery. Clouds had moved in, obscuring some of the stars, which meant it was even darker than it had been the night before. Longarm knew where he was going, though. By now he was pretty familiar with the layout of the Lodestone cemetery.

After climbing over the wall, he stayed beside it, circling toward the shed near the entrance. With a storm possibly coming in, it was unlikely that Lonnie would be sleeping behind the shed. The caretaker might be inside it, though. Longarm planned to check. He wasn't going to be taken by surprise this time.

When he came in sight of the shed, he stopped short and frowned. The door was open. The hinges creaked as it blew back and forth in the rising wind. The stygian darkness inside the shed made the door look a little like a mouth opening and closing, a black maw that was ready to engulf anyone foolish enough to come near it.

Longarm paused only for a moment, and then with drawn gun, he eased around to the back of the shed. If Lonnie was there, Longarm planned to knock him out and tie him up.

Lonnie wasn't there, though. Longarm poked around noiselessly in the shadows until he was satisfied of that.

That left the inside of the shed.

He circled around to the front, took a deep breath, and went in fast and low, crouching with the Colt ready in his hand. No one challenged him. Utter silence filled the little building.

Longarm pulled the door to and held it closed. He didn't want even the faintest glow to escape when he struck a match. As the lucifer flared up, he squinted around the inside of the shed.

It was empty except for the lanterns and the tools. Only one shovel leaned against the wall, but one was all Longarm needed. He dropped the match, ground out the little flame, and picked up the shovel.

On the map of the cemetery that he carried in his head

he had marked the location of all the suspicious graves. When he left the shed, he knew where he was going. He closed the door behind him and fastened it. He didn't want it slamming in the wind and drawing any attention up here.

As he moved across the graveyard, the wind blew harder and chillier. The smell of rain was stronger. He frowned and hoped that the storm would hold off for a while. The idea of digging up graves in a pouring rain wasn't very appealing.

On the other hand, he thought, if it was raining, then folks would be even less likely to come up here. They would stay snug in their homes, not even giving any thought to what might be going on up at the graveyard.

He didn't spend a lot of time worrying about it. It would either rain or it wouldn't, and there wasn't a damned thing he could do about it.

Silver Jack Meehan's grave would be the easiest to open, since it was the newest. He headed for it, but before he got there, a sound came to his ears that made him freeze in his tracks. The way the wind was whipping around as he stood there and listened intently, sometimes he heard the noise and sometimes he didn't. He heard enough to recognize that scraping, rasping sound, though.

Somebody was digging.

Chapter 21

So he wasn't alone in the graveyard after all. And that explained why there had been only one shovel inside the shed. Somebody had taken the other one and was working industriously with it now.

Lonnie? He was the caretaker of the cemetery, but he would have no legitimate reason to be working on a grave at this time of night, in the dark, with a storm approaching.

Flynn? If he was as villainous as Longarm believed him to be, then he wouldn't have any reason to dig up a grave. He would want them left alone.

Nor could Longarm think of why anybody else from Lodestone would be up here skulking around and digging in the dark. He couldn't ignore the mystery, though, so he began making his way quietly toward the spot where the digging sounds seemed to originate, judging as best he could in the inconsistant wind.

As he drew nearer, the sounds became louder, to the point that he could hear them even over the rustling of the tree branches. He heard something else, too, something that made him pause again.

He couldn't be sure, but he thought it sounded like somebody . . . crying.

Longarm's jaw clenched and he muttered a curse as he

figured out who was up here with him. He wasn't sure how the thing had been managed, but like it or not, he would have to deal with the problem.

He started forward again, and after a moment he was able to see the slender figure leaning over one of the graves, shovel in hand. Longarm recalled who was supposed to be buried there, and that was the clincher.

Quickly, he stepped forward and came up beside the person digging. He reached out, grabbed the shovel, and said, "Caroline, what the hell are you doing here?"

She gave a muffled scream and jerked around toward him. She let go of the shovel she had been using, but only so that she could ball her hands into small fists and start punching at Longarm. Those fists thudded against his chest until he dropped both shovels and caught hold of her wrists, clamping down hard enough to stop her from attacking him without really hurting her.

"Caroline, take it easy!" he told her in a low, urgent voice. "It's me, Custis Long!"

She stopped fighting suddenly and gasped, "Custis?" Then she sagged in his grip, swayed forward, and pressed her face against his chest. He felt the tears on her cheeks dampening his shirt.

"Caroline, you shouldn't be here," he said as he held her, feeling the tiny shudders that went through her body.

"But . . . but I had to come!" she said. "I had to know. My father's still alive, isn't he?" She lifted her head and tilted it back so that she could look up into his face, even though in the deep darkness neither of them could see the other all that well. "Isn't he?"

Longarm realized it wasn't going to do any good to lie to her. She was already here where she shouldn't be.

"I think there's at least a chance he is," he said. "What did you do, figure it out after I left Trickham?"

"That's right." She bunched a fist and struck him in the chest again, not out of panic at being startled in the middle

152

of a dark graveyard this time, but because she was angry. In an accusatory tone, she went on, "You knew all along! You should have told me!"

"I didn't *know* anything," Longarm said. "Matter of fact, I still don't. I've got some pretty strong suspicions, but that's all."

"You knew that the theory you laid out about Hathaway paying off Marshal Flynn to make it look like he was dead would apply to my father's case just as well. But you didn't tell me that. You let me figure it out for myself the next day, after you were already gone."

Longarm shrugged. "I was hoping the idea wouldn't come to you until after you'd left on the train. I planned to let you know what I found out when I came back here to Lodestone, though."

"When were you going to tell me? When it would be too late for me to ever find my father?"

"I thought I might give you a hand with that chore, too, if I could talk my boss into it."

"I . . . I don't know whether to believe you or not, Custis. But I'm still mad at you, regardless."

"What did you do," he asked, "rent that buggy again and follow me over here?"

"No, I rented a saddle horse this time." He had already noticed that she was wearing trousers and a man's shirt. Behind her head a Stetson hung from its chin strap. "I didn't have the patience to use a buggy."

"Where'd you learn to ride that well?"

"I've been riding practically all my life. I even worked at a stable in Omaha for a while."

Longarm grunted. "You're a gal who's just full of surprises, Caroline."

Her chin jutted defiantly. "I don't like being underestimated."

"I won't make that mistake twice," Longarm said dryly.

"I think you already have. At least twice."

He chuckled, but then grew serious again. "So you planned to dig up what's supposed to be your pa's grave and see whether or not he's in it, is that right?"

Despite her resolve, her voice trembled a little as she replied, "That's right."

"I'll give you a hand. I'd planned on digging up Silver Jack Meehan's grave since it's fresher, but I reckon this one will do."

"Silver Jack Meehan?" Caroline repeated. "The outlaw that the deputy over in Trickham asked you about?"

"That's right. According to Marshal Flynn, he got kicked in the head by a bad horse and killed a couple of days ago. He's supposed to be buried right down yonder." Longarm waved toward the newest grave in the cemetery.

"Supposed to be."

"Yep. Them's what you call the operative words." Longarm bent and picked up one of the shovels. "Stand back, and I'll get to work on this."

"I'll help you," Caroline said. "There's no reason both of us can't dig."

Longarm was about to protest out of chivalrous habit, but then he realized that she was right. If they both dug, the chore would go a lot faster.

The shovels bit into the earth, flinging the dirt to both sides of the grave. As they worked, Longarm explained to Caroline everything that he had worked out about the nefarious goings-on in Lodestone.

"You make it sound like the whole town is in on it!" she said.

"Nope, not the whole town. Just Flynn, Mayor Bascomb, Edgar Horne the undertaker, and Doc Donaldson. I ain't sure about Bascomb and the doc, but the way I see it, Horne would have to be part of the plot if it was going to work. He's the unofficial coroner in these parts. Having the doc in on the game would make it easier, too, and I reckon I suspect Bascomb just because he's such an ornery son of a gun."

"Son of a bitch is more like it," muttered Caroline. "After all, he sired a royal bastard."

Longarm grinned. "He did, at that. And it could be that Riley knows what's going on, too. But I figure that's probably the extent of it. If anybody else in town suspects that there's something fishy about all those owlhoots showing up and mysteriously dying, well, they're keeping their mouths shut about it. It's only natural that they wouldn't want to believe the hombres running the town are crooks."

The hole was getting pretty deep now. Longarm climbed down inside it while Caroline stayed on top. It was so dark in the grave that Longarm had to work by feel. Some lantern light would have been helpful, but they couldn't risk it.

"Had to take a lot of nerve, sneaking into a cemetery after dark like you did," he said.

"A lot of nerve for a girl, you mean?"

"A lot of nerve for anybody." He paused and looked up at the branches whipping around in the wind. "It's mighty spooky in here tonight."

"I don't care about that," Caroline said. "I just want to know if my father is really buried here, or if he's still alive somewhere."

"You know that if he really is here . . . it ain't going to be pleasant." Longarm grimaced as he remembered what it had been like opening Nate Hathaway's coffin.

"I know," Caroline said, and he could tell that she was making an effort to keep her voice steady. "But I still have to be sure, one way or the other."

The shovel hit something solid as Longarm pushed it into the dirt. "We'll know before too much longer."

It still took him a while, though, to clear away the dirt from the top of the coffin. Nobody could complain about the job Lonnie did as a gravedigger. He planted 'em plenty deep.

When Longarm had the lid uncovered, he thumped the shovel blade against it. "Sounds a little hollow," he said.

"Like there's nothing in there."

"Yeah. But there's only one way to be sure. You ready?"

He heard her take a deep breath and then say, "Go ahead."

Just as he had the previous night, he worked the shovel blade under the lid and pried upward on it. Again the nails resisted but finally gave way. Longarm braced himself as the lid came up, not really expecting the stench of a decomposing body but knowing that it might be there anyway.

As he stood there for a long moment, though, nothing came out of the coffin except for a faint smell of damp wood.

"Custis . . . ?" Caroline asked, unable to keep the quiver out of her voice.

"I think it's empty," he told her. "Hang on a minute."

Crouched here well below ground level, he thought he could risk a small light. He took a lucifer out of his pocket and scratched it to life on the coffin lid. Flame spurted from the tip. The glare from the match fell on the empty coffin. There was nothing inside it except the black cloth with which it was lined.

"Reckon you can add Lonnie to the list of folks who know what's going on," Longarm said. "He couldn't handle these coffins without knowing there was nobody inside them. But he's slow-witted enough that he's probably just been doing whatever Flynn tells him to do."

Caroline knelt beside the empty grave. "What are you going to do now? Should we dig up some more of them, just to be sure?"

"This is proof enough for me. What I want you to do is get out of here, find your horse, and ride back over to Trickham as fast as you can. Tell the deputy what's going on and have him get a posse together, just in case."

"What are you going to be doing?"

"Flynn don't know I came back to Lodestone again. I hope to get the drop on him and lock him up in his own jail. Then, one by one, I'll grab the rest of the bunch and put them behind bars, too."

"You're going after the whole gang by yourself?"

"Don't have much choice. Once Flynn sees that somebody's tampered with this grave, he'll know that the jig is up. He's probably been stashing the payoffs he gets from the owlhoots. He'll grab the loot and run. That's why I've got to take him by surprise tonight."

Caroline's voice was worried as she said, "I don't like it. It's too dangerous for you."

"It won't be if I handle it right and take them one at a time, like I said."

"But it'll take at least a couple of days for help to get back here from Trickham, and that's if I ride all night and so does the posse."

"Tell Duncan to wire the sheriff in San Angelo. That's closer."

"Not by much."

"We're wasting time," Longarm said. "The sooner you get started riding, the sooner help will get back here if I need it."

Caroline sighed in resignation. "I know, you're right. But I don't have to like it."

"Nobody said you did." Longarm tossed the shovel out of the grave. "Give me a hand climbing out of here before you go." He reached up toward her.

They clasped wrists, and Longarm started to pull himself up out of the hole in the earth. As he emerged from the grave, lightning flashed overhead, its electric glare illuminating the cemetery for a split second.

That heartbeat of light was enough to reveal to Longarm the menacing figure of Marshal Artemus Flynn, standing about twenty feet away with a rifle pointed right at them.

Chapter 22

Longarm gave Caroline a hard shove that sent her stumbling backward, and then he threw himself in the opposite direction as flame lanced from the muzzle of Flynn's rifle. The slug smacked between them and whistled off into the cemetery.

If there had been any doubt in Longarm's mind that Flynn was on the wrong side of the law, it was gone now. The man had just tried to kill them.

Even as he hit the ground, Longarm was palming his Colt from the cross-draw rig. He rolled onto his belly and triggered twice in the direction where Flynn had been standing.

After that flash of lightning, darkness had closed in again and seemed darker than ever, so Longarm had no idea if Flynn was still in the same place. It didn't seem likely. Flynn was smart enough to have moved after he fired.

So was Longarm. The big lawman rolled again.

The earth suddenly opened up underneath him, and as he fell Longarm realized that he had rolled right into Gordon Thaxter's so-called final resting place. He landed in the coffin itself, bruising his knees against the hard wood.

His normally icy nerves were stretched taut. The approaching storm, the surroundings, the danger, and now the idea of lying in a coffin, even one that had never been occupied, made Longarm's insides jerk and jangle. Biting back the yell that wanted to rise in his throat, he pushed himself upright and scrambled out of the grave, keeping low.

But not low enough to avoid being seen as lightning flickered again. Flynn's rifle blasted. The bullet whined over Longarm's head and smashed into Gordon Thaxter's phony marker, showering Longarm with splinters. He snapped a shot at Flynn's muzzle flash and hoped that Caroline had the sense to find one of the marble tombstones, crawl behind it, and stay there.

He cursed himself for underestimating Flynn. Maybe the marshal hadn't stood guard up here all evening—and Longarm had no way of knowing that—but at the very least Flynn had come up to the cemetery to check it out before turning in. He must have heard Longarm and Caroline talking and tried to sneak up on them.

He would have succeeded, too, if not for that fortuitous lightning flash. If that hadn't happened when it did, Longarm had a feeling he and Caroline would have wound up in that grave permanently.

It might still happen. Flynn was out there somewhere in the darkness, stalking them.

On his belly, Longarm crawled away from Thaxter's grave. He didn't have to worry too much about the noises he made; the wind would cover them up so that Flynn couldn't hear them. The lightning was the real threat. If it flashed again, Flynn might see him.

But that worked both ways. Longarm needed the lightning to pin down Flynn's location, too.

While he was waiting, he slipped fresh cartridges from the loops on his shell belt, opened the Colt's cylinder, and replaced the rounds he had already fired. Normally the hammer rested on an empty chamber, but not tonight. Longarm loaded all six and figured he would need them before the night was over.

When the next lightning flash came, he was ready for it and looked around as much as he could, hoping to spot Flynn. He didn't see the marshal anywhere, though. Flynn must have gone to ground, too.

But as the thunder that inevitably followed the lightning rumbled over the hillside, Longarm heard another sound blended with it that turned his blood to ice in his veins.

Caroline screamed.

Flynn had her. That was the only explanation. Caroline wasn't the sort of gal who let out a scream just because of some thunder and lightning.

As the echoes of the thunderclap faded, Longarm surged up off the ground and hurried toward the sound of Caroline's brief outcry. It had cut off in mid-shriek, as if somebody had clapped a hand over her mouth—or something worse.

He ran into a couple of tombstones, bruising himself even more, but he bounced off and kept going. The lightning came again, the split-second glare revealing two struggling figures about fifteen feet away, off to Longarm's right. He veered toward them but didn't slow down. Quickly, he holstered his revolver so that he would have both hands free, and then a second later he crashed into the people who were wrestling with each other.

The collision knocked everybody sprawling. Longarm rolled over, came up on hands and knees, and reached out blindly. His fingers brushed cloth. Somebody grunted in surprise and twisted toward him. A fist came out of the darkness and scraped the side of Longarm's head. He powered forward with his legs, spreading his arms to wrap them around his opponent.

The muscular feel of the unseen enemy's body told Longarm that he hadn't tackled Caroline by mistake. He got his left hand on the man's throat and drove his right fist just above it, into the hombre's face. Longarm figured this was Flynn he was fighting with, but the crooked marshal might have had some allies out here that Longarm hadn't seen yet.

161

It didn't really matter. Longarm's only friend in this graveyard was Caroline; anybody else he encountered was an enemy.

The man heaved his body off the ground and threw Longarm to the side. Pouncing like a cat, the man landed on top of the federal lawman, and this time it was Longarm's turn to feel a choking grip close around his throat.

He brought his knee up, aiming blindly, but from the howl of pain when the blow landed, he knew he had found his opponent's groin. The hands that had been locked on Longarm's throat came free. Longarm shoved the man off him.

Seizing the momentary advantage, Longarm threw himself on the enemy and began hooking punches to the man's midsection. Again and again Longarm's powerful fists drove into belly and solar plexus. When Longarm finally pushed himself up, the man he had been pummeling lay huddled on the ground, a broken, whimpering mass.

He risked a shout. "Caroline! Caroline, where are you?"

The frantic reply came from his left. "Over here, Custis, over here!"

Longarm swung in that direction, but as he did so, lightning flashed and thunder boomed again—only it wasn't really thunder and lightning but rather the close-range blast of a gun. What felt like a huge fist smashed into the top of his left shoulder and knocked him backward. He knew the bullet had clipped him. His whole left arm went numb as he lost his balance and fell to the ground.

So Flynn *did* have allies out here. There was barely time for that thought to flash through Longarm's brain before more shots erupted. Colt flame stabbed toward him as he rolled desperately to the side with no chance to draw his own gun. All he could do was try to avoid the bullets thudding into the ground scant inches away.

He bumped into a tombstone and wriggled behind it. Marble dust rained down on him as bullets smashed into the stone above his head.

Then the gunman's bullets ran out and a sudden silence

fell over the cemetery, broken only by the moaning of the wind. Longarm reached for his Colt but froze as his fingers touched the revolver's walnut grips. He couldn't start blazing away in the darkness. Caroline was out there somewhere, probably not too far away. If he opened fire, he ran too high a risk of hitting her by accident.

Once again he had to wait for the enemy to come to him.

The minutes stretched out agonizingly as Longarm crouched behind the tombstone. He didn't know if Caroline was a prisoner or if she had managed to get away. He hoped she could elude the bastards, get out of the cemetery, find her horse, and ride like hell away from here.

That was pretty unlikely, though, and he knew it. Even if she hadn't been caught by whoever was out there, his instincts told him that she wouldn't abandon him. She would want to stay and try to help him.

"Long! Marshal Long! You hear me?"

The shout that lifted over the wind came from Flynn. He sounded all right, so Longarm knew the man he had beaten into a semi-conscious state hadn't been the marshal. Nor had the man been big enough to be Lonnie, or soft enough to be Mayor Bascomb. Longarm wasn't sure who that left. Edgar Horne, maybe.

He didn't care. Flynn was the mastermind behind all this trouble. Flynn was the most dangerous of his enemies.

"Long, damn it, answer me!"

Longarm didn't answer. He crouched there in silence, unwilling to give away his position. He could have triggered a couple of rounds toward the sound of Flynn's voice, but that would reveal his location, too, and he couldn't be sure that Flynn wasn't using Caroline as a human shield.

As if he had read Longarm's thoughts, Flynn shouted, "Long, I've got the girl!"

A second later Caroline cried out in pain, demonstrating that Flynn wasn't lying. In a strained voice, she called, "He . . . he's telling the truth, Custis!"

Longarm's teeth ground together hard as he fought down the impulse to yell curses at Flynn. On hands and knees he crawled silently from behind the tombstone.

"Long, you'd better speak up, or I'm going to hurt her! Throw down your gun, put your hands up, and walk toward the sound of my voice, or by God I'll kill her!"

Longarm didn't think Flynn would kill Caroline. If he did, then he wouldn't be able to use her as leverage anymore. Flynn was smart enough to know how valuable she was as a bargaining chip.

But if he wanted to keep hollering threats, that was just fine. The sound of his voice told Longarm where he was.

Moving quickly but quietly, Longarm crawled through the cemetery, circling toward Flynn's position.

Caroline suddenly screamed in pain again, a cry that dwindled away into a series of whimpers. Flynn called, "I don't know if you heard the snap or not, but that was one of her fingers breaking, Long! I'll break another one in thirty seconds if you haven't surrendered by then!"

It was all Longarm could do not to leap up and charge the son of a bitch. He didn't doubt for a second that Flynn had actually broken Caroline's finger. Flynn knew that it wouldn't be smart to kill her—but he could put her through a hell of a lot of pain.

Without thinking about it, Longarm was counting off the seconds in his head. He hoped Flynn wouldn't carry out his threat, but when thirty seconds had passed another shriek echoed through the graveyard.

"That's two fingers broken, Long! But the girl has eight more!"

Longarm estimated that he wasn't more than twenty feet from Flynn now. He needed to get a little closer, though, because when he struck it would have to be fast. After crawling several more feet, he hunkered behind one of the bushes that dotted the cemetery and waited for another lightning flash. He had to be able to see what he was doing.

The numbness caused by the bullet nicking his shoulder

had faded from his left arm, so he could use it again. His shoulder ached, but he could live with that pain. He gathered his legs under him, ready to burst into the open.

With a series of little thuds, heavy raindrops began to strike the ground. Longarm heard them hitting the leaves in the trees, too. The rain was finally here. Where was the lightning?

When the next flash finally came, he peered through slitted eyes and saw Flynn and Caroline standing no more than a dozen feet from him at the foot of a grave. Even though the lightning lasted only a split second, the scene imprinted itself on Longarm's brain.

Flynn had his left arm looped tightly and cruelly around Caroline's neck. She struggled against him, but feebly, as if she were on the verge of passing out. In his right hand Flynn held a revolver. His head jerked from side to side as he looked around, trying to find any sign of the man he wanted so badly to kill.

Longarm still couldn't risk a shot. He would rush in, swing his pistol at Flynn's head, and try to knock out the crooked marshal before Flynn could get a shot off or do anything to hurt Caroline again. Almost before the lightning flash began to fade, Longarm leaped from behind the bush and threw himself forward at Flynn.

Too late, he sensed as much as heard something whistling through the air toward his head. He was already moving too fast to stop or swerve aside.

With a terrible crash something slammed into the side of his head and toppled him off his feet. He landed hard on the ground and rolled over so that several fat drops of rain splattered into his face. He felt them falling on him like giant tears . . .

Then he didn't feel anything anymore, and if the lightning flashed and the thunder rolled, he never knew it. Oblivion had claimed him.

Chapter 23

The first thing he was aware of when consciousness seeped back into his brain was a steady, almost rhythmic pounding. It took him a while before he realized that it was the sound of rain hitting a roof. A tin roof, to judge from the racket it was making.

The rain wasn't falling on him, so he decided he must be inside a building somewhere. That was better than he had expected. In that awful instant just before he passed out, he had fully expected to never wake up. Flynn would kill him and Caroline both.

But obviously, he wasn't dead yet, Longarm told himself. And that meant there was still hope . . .

He kept his eyes closed and didn't move as he tried to take stock of the situation. His head hung forward. His arms were pulled back, and he couldn't move them. He was sitting on something—a chair, that was it—and his legs were tied to it, as well as his arms. That explained why he couldn't move.

His clothes were wet. He had been out in the rain and had been dragged in here, wherever here was. His first thought was that Flynn and his accomplices had put him and Caroline in the shed just inside the cemetery, but after mulling it over he discarded that idea. There hadn't been a

167

chair in the shed like the one he was tied to, and the shed didn't have a tin roof, either. He was somewhere else.

He wondered if Caroline was with him.

Carefully, he opened his eyes the tiniest fraction of an inch. Even through that narrow slit, the light from a lantern was bright enough to batter at him and nearly make him flinch. With an effort of will, he controlled the reaction and waited while his eyesight gradually adjusted.

With his head tipped forward, he couldn't see anything except the rough planks of the floor. He listened intently and thought he heard breathing to his left. After a moment he heard a faint whimper and knew someone was there. The noise had sounded pained, so he thought there was a good chance it came from Caroline. She had to be in agony from those two broken fingers.

Artemus Flynn would pay for that, the bastard, vowed Longarm. Even though he was in no position to take any sort of vengeance on Flynn at the moment, he made the promise to himself anyway.

A door opened. Footsteps sounded. Longarm didn't have to worry anymore about pretending to be unconscious, because somebody grabbed his hair, jerked his head up, and cracked a vicious slap across his face.

"Wake up, Long. Wake up, you son of a bitch."

Longarm tasted blood in his mouth. He opened his eyes and peered blearily up at the hate-contorted face of Riley Bascomb.

Riley's presence came as something of a shock. He was supposed to be locked up over in Trickham. Obviously, he had gotten out of jail somehow, and the fact that he was here meant that he was part of Flynn's scheme, just as Longarm had suspected he might be.

With a grimace, Riley pressed a hand to his belly. "Feels like you busted me up really bad inside, you bastard," he said. "I'm gonna enjoy killin' you."

So it had been Riley that Longarm had pounded into

senselessness back in the cemetery. The young man's face was pale and drawn, and he moved like he was in pain.

Longarm hoped Riley's belly hurt like hell.

He looked to his left and saw that Caroline was tied to a chair, too. Her auburn hair had gotten wet and now hung in damp ringlets around her face. She was awake and looked over at Longarm with concern in her eyes, as well as the pain from her injured hand.

"Custis, are you all right?" she asked. "I was afraid Horne fractured your skull with that shovel."

"So it was Horne who hit me?" Longarm said thickly. "I didn't know who did it."

"He was waiting behind a tombstone. I didn't see him in time to warn you. I'm not sure I could have said anything anyway, the way Flynn was choking me." In fact, her voice was still hoarse.

"This ol' noggin of mine is pretty much hard as iron," said Longarm, "so don't worry about me. How's your hand?"

She smiled wanly. "It hurts. But broken fingers can be set."

Riley suddenly exclaimed, "What the hell is wrong with you two? You're talking like you're gonna get out of here! Hell, you ain't gonna live to see the morning!"

"Hide and watch, old son," Longarm said. "We ain't dead yet."

Riley gave a disgusted snort. "You'd already be dead if it was up to me."

The door behind him had opened as he spoke, and Flynn came into the room in time to hear the comment. He said sharply, "It's not up to you, though, now is it?"

Water dripped off the brim of his hat and the yellow slicker that he wore. A short, plump figure followed him in. Mayor Hugh Bascomb wore an expensive hat and raincoat. The third and final man to come into the room was the short, wiry Edgar Horne, Lodestone's undertaker, also in a slicker. He shut the door behind them.

Longarm looked around. They were in a single-room cabin somewhere. It was spartanly furnished, with a rough-hewn table, a few chairs, a rope bunk, and a cast-iron stove in one corner. Rain pelted against the lone window beside the door. Hugh Bascomb and Edgar Horne went over to the stove and held their hands out toward it, trying to dry their clothes and ward off a chill. Riley joined them.

Flynn took his hat off and shook water from it as he came over to stand in front of Longarm and Caroline. He said, "I'm truly sorry that I had to cause you so much pain, Miss Thaxter. If Marshal Long had cooperated, it might not have been so bad."

"Save your apologies, Marshal," Caroline said. Despite the discomfort she felt, the sight of their enemies had brought some spirit back into her voice. She went on, "You're planning to kill us, aren't you?"

Flynn shrugged and put his hat back on. "Pretty much have to," he said. "But we'll make it as quick and painless as possible."

"Not for that bastard Long, though," Riley said from the stove. "He's got to suffer for what he did to me."

"Like I said, that's not your decision to make," Flynn told him.

Bascomb spoke up. "Maybe Riley should have a say in these things, Artemus. He's helped us out before. I think it's time he was made a full partner in our little enterprise."

"That's just your way of increasing your share of the take," Horne said. "You ain't satisfied with a three-way split like the rest of us."

With a frown, Bascomb blustered, "That's not true. I just think it's only fair to include Riley. He's running risks just like the rest of us, you know."

"He's a young fool who'd still be behind bars if you hadn't pulled so many strings and called in every favor that's owed you, Hugh," Flynn said caustically. "You and Edgar and I went into this arrangement as partners, and that's the way it's going to stay."

His tone didn't allow for any argument. Bascomb subsided, but not without some grumbling first. Riley looked mad and unhappy, too.

That was interesting, Longarm told himself. Anything that could drive a wedge between a man's enemies might turn out to be handy.

In the meantime, and to postpone the fate that Flynn intended for them, he wanted some answers. He asked, "Where are we?"

"An old trapper's cabin on top of Lodestone Mountain," Flynn replied. "That's the big hill that overlooks the town. Nobody ever comes up here but us, Marshal, in case you were thinking somebody might come along to help you."

"No, I didn't figure on that," Longarm said honestly. "I'm a mite curious why you brought us up here, though."

"To get rid of you, of course."

"How come you didn't just shoot us and toss us in that hole where Miss Thaxter's pa was supposed to be buried?"

"There had already been too much shooting in the cemetery tonight," Flynn said. "I doubt if anyone heard the gunfire over the sound of the storm, but it's possible. I didn't want to take a chance on attracting any attention."

Longarm smiled humorlessly. "You mean you don't want the folks who live in Lodestone to know that their marshal's nothing but a small-time crook, along with their mayor and the undertaker?"

"There's nothing small-time about what we've been doing," Bascomb said resentfully. "We've made plenty of money at it. More money than a man like you will ever see, Long."

"You're probably right, considering that I come by my wages honest-like, instead of helping a bunch of owlhoots escape from the law by pretending to be dead."

Riley laughed harshly, and Bascomb and Horne smiled. Flynn was the only one who didn't seem to think what Longarm had just said was funny. He said, "Is that what you think we've been doing, Marshal?"

171

Longarm was cold from the wet clothes he wore, but at Flynn's words a chill went through him that had nothing to do with dampness. He looked at the crooked lawman and said quietly, "Well, son of a bitch."

"Marshal Flynn," Caroline said, "do you know where my father really is?"

He looked over at her and nodded solemnly. "As a matter of fact, Miss Thaxter, I do. He's buried right out back, in the woods behind this cabin, along with all the other outlaws who came to Lodestone thinking that they would escape the justice they deserved."

Chapter 24

Caroline gasped at Flynn's blunt words, as if he had struck her across the face. In a way he had, because he had just dashed the last hope she had of ever seeing her father alive again.

She turned her head to stare in confusion at Longarm. "Custis, I don't understand . . ."

"I reckon I do," Longarm said grimly. "Let me see if I've got the straight of it now, Flynn. You spread the word that wanted outlaws could come to Lodestone and supposedly die and be buried here, so they could go somewhere else and get a fresh start, in return for a share of their loot."

"That's right," Flynn acknowledged.

"But they didn't really ride on. You and your partners here killed them and kept all the loot, not just a share of it."

"You can't convince me that you really feel sorry for them, Marshal. They were all wanted men. Most of them were killers. They got what they had coming to them."

A little sob escaped from Caroline.

"Why go to the trouble of burying them up here?" asked Longarm. "Why the charade of burying empty coffins down in the cemetery?"

"We were dealing with desperate men," Flynn explained. "Men who lived as long as they did by being care-

173

ful. The first few insisted on seeing for themselves that the empty coffins were buried and the markers put up as agreed. They wanted to get their money's worth. I knew about this isolated cabin, so I came up with the idea of meeting here for the payoff. By that time, all their suspicions had been allayed, so it was easy to take them by surprise and dispose of them. We buried them up here because it was easier than taking them back down the hill to the cemetery. After that . . ." Flynn smiled faintly. "Well, call it habit, I suppose. When something works, you're reluctant to change it."

"You had to with Nate Hathaway, though," Longarm said pointedly.

Flynn's smile disappeared, to be replaced by an angry grimace. "Calvin Johnson, you mean, because that's who he was to us. We had no idea who he really was. He came into town, got sick, and died from a fever, just as I told you. It came as a complete surprise when you told me who he really was." Flynn shook his head. "When I think about that army payroll we'll never lay our hands on, it just makes me sick."

Longarm stared at him for a moment and then began to laugh. "So that's why you didn't mind me digging him up. You knew he was really where he was supposed to be. That was a neat trick fate played on you, all right. I never would have uncovered this whole scheme if I hadn't trailed Hathaway to Lodestone."

"Well, it doesn't matter," snapped Flynn. "You're going to die, and we'll carry on just as we have been. Nothing will change."

Longarm nodded toward the three men by the stove. "Except you'll have to split four ways from now on instead of three, if you make Riley a partner, too." He asked the mayor, "What did you do, Bascomb, send a fast rider to Trickham as soon as you found out your boy was in jail there?"

"That's right," Bascomb answered defiantly. "I was damned if I was going to leave him behind bars. The sheriff of Coleman County and I are old friends. I was able to persuade him that Riley was being railroaded on trumped-up charges. Marshal Flynn wrote a note backing me up on that. As soon as Riley was released, he got back over here as fast as he could."

"I'll bet that sheriff don't know what a crooked bastard you really are."

Bascomb's face flushed with rage. "My God, can't you see that we're performing a *service*? We're ridding the frontier of vicious outlaws!"

"If you have to look at it like that so you can sleep at night, then so be it, old son. To me, though, you're nothing but a bunch of thieves and murderers."

Flynn put his hand on the butt of his gun. "This isn't getting us anywhere."

"What about the doc?" Longarm asked hastily. "Is he part of the scheme, too?"

Flynn made a noise. Longarm couldn't tell if it was a grunt or a chuckle. "Hobart Donaldson is the easiest sort of man to deal with . . . an honest man with a shameful secret. He was drunk one night when he tried to deliver a baby. The mother and child both died. Doc will do anything we tell him to do in order to keep that secret from coming out."

Even as Flynn spoke, the door opened wider behind him. Longarm had seen it start to open when he asked the question about Donaldson, just as he had seen the man's face peering in through the window a moment before that.

The doctor stood there, a horrified look on his pale, stricken face. None of the other four men had noticed him. They didn't even know the door was open until a gust of wind blew some rain splattering into the room.

When that happened, though, they all turned abruptly toward the door—only to freeze when they saw the double-barreled shotgun clutched in Hobart Donaldson's hands.

"What are you doing?" Donaldson asked in a shaky voice. "That man's a federal marshal!"

"All the more reason why we have to take care of him, Doc," Flynn said in a calm, reasonable voice. "You know we can't have anybody finding out what's been going on."

With an irritated expression on his fleshy face, Hugh Bascomb went over and shut the door. "Damn it, Hobart, what are you doing up here?" he demanded. "We don't need your help on this job."

"Job?" Donaldson laughed harshly. "This murder, you mean! When I saw all of you leaving town, I figured you were coming up here, but I never dreamed you were going to kill a U.S. marshal and an innocent woman!"

With a sneer on his face, Riley said, "Don't get so high and mighty about it, you quack sawbones. At least we don't butcher folks because we're drunk."

Donaldson swung the greener toward Riley, making the young man curse and step back quickly. "You kill people because you're greedy and evil," he accused. "That's even worse. And . . . and Lord help me, I've gone along with you."

"And been well paid for it, I might add," Bascomb said.

"No more! This is it, you understand? It's all over."

"Hobart—" Flynn began, still trying to sound calm.

Donaldson put his back against the door so that he could cover the whole room with the shotgun. "Cut them loose!" he cried. "Damn it, cut them loose or I'll shoot!"

"If you fire that thing in here, you're liable to hit Long and the woman, too," Horne pointed out. "It's mighty close quarters in here, Doc. Why don't you put the shotgun down?" A grin spread across the undertaker's face. "I got a bottle in my coat pocket. We'll have a few nips, warm our blood up a mite. What do you say?"

Donaldson had been wavering, but the callous offer of a drink made up his mind for him. It infuriated him, in fact, and the anger seemed to steady his nerves. The twin barrels of the scattergun stopped shaking quite so much.

"Cut them loose," he repeated quietly. "Or I swear, nobody will leave this place alive."

Flynn's face hardened, and Longarm knew the crooked marshal wasn't going to give up. He would risk everything on a fast draw and a quick shot before he'd do that.

Bascomb wasn't made of such stern stuff, though. The threat of a double load of buckshot would put water in most men's knees, and the mayor of Lodestone was no exception. Abruptly, he cried out, "For God's sake, Donaldson, don't shoot!" He pulled a clasp knife from his pocket and started forward. "I'll cut them loose, just be careful with that shotgun!"

"Hugh, don't—" Flynn said, but before he could go on, Riley took a hand. His gun came out in a slick move and pointed at Flynn.

"Stop tellin' everybody what to do," he said. "You think you're too damn good to give me a share. Think you can lord it over everybody just because you're the marshal. Hell, you're an outlaw just like the rest of us!"

"Damn it, boy, think about what you're doing," Flynn warned him.

Longarm looked at the knife in Bascomb's hand. He wanted that knife to cut his bonds before all hell broke loose in this cabin, so that he could take a hand in it and maybe save his life and Caroline's. He said, "Mayor, it seems to me like you and Riley and Horne could run this deal just as easy without Flynn. Hell, you can always appoint another town marshal. That might even be a good job for Riley."

Bascomb came a step closer, bringing the knife tantalizingly closer as well. "Cover Flynn, Riley," he told his son. "Long, what are you talking about?"

"I got no reason to stay around here," Longarm said, trying to sound as sincere as possible. "The job that brought me here is done. I can go back to Denver and forget I ever heard of Lodestone."

"Damn it, he's lying," Flynn objected. "Can't you see—"

"I see a man who's starting to make some sense," Bascomb said. "Riley, keep Flynn covered. Long, what would it take for you to forget about Lodestone, like you said?"

"Oh, I don't know," drawled Longarm. "Ten thousand, maybe."

"Custis!" Caroline exclaimed in shock.

Longarm shrugged as best he could with his arms tied. "Darlin', if you knew what sort of salary a deputy U.S. marshal makes, you wouldn't be a bit surprised."

Bascomb grinned, and Longarm knew he had him. A greedy, evil bastard always assumed that everybody else was as greedy and as evil as he was.

"Five thousand," Bascomb said. "That's as high as we'll go."

"I reckon five will do," agreed Longarm.

"What about the girl?"

Longarm looked over at her. "Who's going to believe her if she tries to say anything? She's just an owlhoot's daughter. Probably a whore back where she comes from."

Caroline began to cry. Longarm hated for her to feel betrayed like this, but her reaction just made it all seem more real.

Bascomb looked over at Horne. "What do you say, Edgar? I think the marshal's badge would look real good on Riley, don't you?"

As long as Riley had the drop on Flynn, there was nothing Horne could do except agree. "Sure, Hugh, whatever you say."

"You're all crazy!" Flynn said hotly. "Long is trying to trick you—"

"I don't think so," Bascomb said. "I think he's just getting smart, like Riley and Edgar and me."

And with that, he bent over and slashed the ropes holding Longarm's legs to the chair. He straightened and started to work on the bonds holding the big lawman's arms.

Hobart Donaldson had watched the proceedings with a look of confusion growing on his face. He had wanted Longarm and Caroline freed, but he obviously hadn't expected the Bascombs and Horne to turn on Flynn. He lowered the shotgun slightly and said, "Wait just a damned minute—"

"Oh, don't be so blasted self-righteous," Bascomb said as he finished sawing through the ropes on the big lawman's arms. "We're not going to kill Marshal Long and Miss Thaxter after all. The only one who's going to die here tonight is Flynn, who started it all in the first place. So you see, you don't have to—"

Bascomb stopped short and dropped the knife in his hand, even as Longarm flexed his arm and leg muscles to get some feeling back into them. Bascomb staggered forward a step, his mouth hanging open. His eyes bulged from their sockets. He gasped and pressed a hand to his chest, then fell to his knees.

"Pa!" Riley shouted in alarm. As he turned toward his father, the gun in his hand swung away from Flynn.

That was all the opening Flynn needed.

His hand flashed to the gun on his hip. It came up spouting flame. Riley had taken one step toward Bascomb, but he was thrown backward by the slugs smashing into his chest. He crashed into the wall, bounced off, and patched to the floor.

Longarm threw himself to the side, toward Caroline. He hit her and the chair and knocked them over. He sprawled on top of her to shield her with his own body as Flynn wheeled toward Donaldson and fired again. The bullet hit the doctor and drove him against the door, but Donaldson's fingers were already on the shotgun's triggers. He jerked them involuntarily as he died, and the double charge of buckshot ripped out of the greener with a tremendous roar.

Horne had been right about it being close quarters in the cabin. So close, in fact, that the charges didn't have time to spread very far before they slammed into Artemus Flynn's face and chest and practically ripped his head off his body. The crooked lawman was a bloody wreck who barely resembled something human when he hit the floor.

From the corner of his eye, Longarm saw Horne clawing under his coat for a gun. Before the undertaker could draw his weapon, Longarm had scooped up Riley's fallen gun and pointed it at him.

"I wouldn't do that if I were you, old son," Longarm told him grimly. "You can still walk out of here alive. That's more than your partners can say."

Horne hesitated, but only for a second. Then he said, "I'm going to take my gun out with two fingers and put it on the floor."

"Go ahead," Longarm told him, "but be mighty careful-like about it."

Horne took out his gun and laid it on the planks at his feet, then kicked it across the room to Longarm. He backed up against the far wall with his hands held high over his head.

"Caroline, are you all right?" Longarm asked. He was pretty sure she hadn't been hit by any of the flying buckshot.

"Yes, I . . . I'm fine," she said. She lay awkwardly on the floor, still tied to the chair. Longarm picked up Bascomb's knife and quickly cut her free. As she sat up and started rubbing her wrists, she said, "You weren't really going to cooperate with them, were you, Custis?"

He smiled. "What do you think?"

"I think I should be ashamed of myself for believing that you would so something like that. Just for the record, though, I didn't appreciate that whore comment."

"Pure fabrication," Longarm said as he helped her to her feet. "Window dressin', I guess you could say."

Hugh Bascomb lay facedown beside his son's body. Longarm hooked a toe under him and rolled him onto his back. Bascomb's bulging eyes stared sightlessly. His face was contorted in lines of agony and disbelief.

"Ticker gave out on him," Horne said. "I've seen it plenty of times in my line of work. I told Hugh he ought to take better care of himself. So did Doc. But he never listened."

"I reckon there are horses outside?"

"Yeah."

"We'll be riding back down to Lodestone," Longarm said. He looked around at the four bodies. "You and Lonnie are going to be busy for the next day or so . . . but this time the coffins won't be empty."

Chapter 25

Horne grumbled all the way down the hill. The rain fell steadily, and lightning still flashed from time to time. The storm seemed to be abating a little, though.

"Are you really gonna make me bury them?" he asked, turning in his saddle to look over his shoulder at Longarm, who rode behind him along with Caroline.

"Damn right. You're the undertaker."

"But you're still going to arrest me anyway? I didn't kill anybody, you know. Flynn did all the killing. All I did was bury empty coffins."

"Reckon that'll keep you from a date with the hangman," said Longarm. "You'll do some prison time, though. Might not be too bad for a man with your skills. Prisons always have graveyards."

"Yeah, there's that," Horne mused.

The trail that led down the hill was hard to follow in the darkness and the rain, but finally the three riders reached the Lodestone cemetery. The rain had tapered off to a drizzle.

"You can spend the night in Flynn's jail," Longarm said as they rode past the cemetery. "I'll deputize some of the men in town to keep an eye on you while you and Lonnie go up and get those bodies tomorrow."

"You know," Horne said, "we had quite a bit of loot

stashed. It could all be yours, Marshal . . . if you'd just forget what happened up there."

"Not hardly," Longarm said. "You're going to jail, Horne." He looked over to see Caroline smiling at him.

That was maybe why it took him a little by surprise when Lonnie came roaring out of the cemetery gate and slammed into him, knocking him out of the saddle.

The hulking caretaker must have been waiting there just inside the cemetery, waiting for Horne to come back down the hill from the actual owlhoots' graveyard. And when he had heard Longarm's comment about Horne going to jail, even Lonnie's less than nimble brain had realized that everything had gone wrong.

Longarm barely had time for those thoughts to flash through his mind before he landed heavily on the muddy ground. Caroline let out a frightened cry as Horne wheeled his horse and yelled, "Kill him, Lonnie! Kill the son of a bitch!"

Lonnie charged around the horse, bent down, grabbed the stunned Longarm, and lifted him like a baby. With an angry roar, Lonnie flung him through the air, right over the fence and into the cemetery. Longarm crashed against one of the tombstones. He cried out as pain shot through his side from a rib that was probably cracked.

He grabbed hold of the tombstone and pulled himself up, knowing that if Lonnie caught him on the ground, the big brute would stomp him to death. A few yards away, Lonnie vaulted the wall and lunged toward him. Longarm ducked away from the charge, grimacing at the pain that shot through him.

He reached for his gun but found only an empty holster. The Colt had fallen out somewhere, and he had no time to look for it. He reached for the derringer in his pocket, but before he could get it out, Lonnie was on him again, wrapping those terrible arms around him in a deadly bear hug.

With his own arms trapped, Longarm did the only thing he could. He drove the crown of his head into Lonnie's face. The big man's nose, already broken from the earlier fight with Longarm, was pulped again by the impact. Lonnie roared in pain, and his grip on Longarm loosened enough so that the lawman was able to get the derringer out of his pocket, shove the twin, over-and-under barrels into Lonnie's open mouth, and pull the triggers.

The double blast blew out the back of Lonnie's skull. Even so, it was a few seconds before death caught up to his nerves and muscles. His arms sagged, and Longarm pulled free and staggered back. Lonnie toppled like a tree.

"Custis!" Caroline screamed.

Lord, did it never end? Longarm bit back a curse and ran toward the cemetery gate. He stopped before he got there, because Horne was just inside the gate, one arm around Caroline's neck. For the second time tonight, she was a prisoner in this graveyard.

Horne had a knife to her throat. Longarm wasn't sure where he had gotten it, but he supposed Horne had had it hidden somewhere in his clothes. As the rain finally came to a stop, Horne said, "Here's what I'm going to do, Marshal. I'm taking the girl with me, and you're not going to follow us or I'll cut her throat. You understand?"

"You said it yourself, Horne," Longarm replied. "You ain't killed anybody. You're not a murderer. But you will be if you kill Miss Thaxter, and I'll never stop until I've hunted you down and seen you hang."

"She'll be fine if you just do as you're told. I want your gun."

"Don't have it," Longarm told him. "It fell out somewhere, probably when Lonnie tossed me over that wall."

"I suppose Lonnie's dead, or you wouldn't be here." Horne shook his head. "Too bad. He was like a good draft horse, though. You can always find another one."

He started backing toward the gate.

The hair on the back of Longarm's neck suddenly stood up. A strange smell prickled his nostrils. He had experienced such sensations before and knew what was about to happen. Desperately, he yelled, "Horne, let her go! The lightning—"

There was no time to complete the warning. A brilliant finger of electrical fury clawed down out of the heavens, the last gasp of the storm that was passing, and it struck the wrought iron gate that was less than a yard away from Horne's back. Horne and Caroline both screamed. She twisted and drove an elbow into his body, knocking herself free from his grasp and causing him to stagger against the gate. The lightning bolt ripped through him as well, only for a split second, but that was more than long enough. He flopped onto the ground with seemingly every muscle in his body jerking.

Longarm dashed forward and knelt beside Caroline, who had fallen to the ground. He caught her up in his arms. "Caroline! Are you all right?"

"I . . . I think so," she gasped. "The lightning . . . the lightning didn't strike me. But Horne . . . ?"

Longarm reached over and felt for a pulse in Horne's neck, and found none. "Dead," he said.

Caroline looked up at him. "Then who's going to . . . take care of burying everyone?"

Longarm looked back at her for a second and then began to laugh. After a moment she started laughing, too, and they sat there like that in the muddy graveyard, surrounded by tombstones, holding on to each other as the storm moved on, the lightning performed the last swirling steps of its dance in the clouds, and the peals of thunder trailed away until they were nothing more than fading echoes of distant drums.

Watch for

**LONGARM AND THE
SWEETHEART VENDETTA**

the 333rd novel in the exciting LONGARM
series from Jove

Coming in August!

LONGARM

**Explore the exciting Old West with one
of the men who made it wild!**